Stormy Seas

Triumphs and Tragedies of Great Lakes Ships

By Wes Oleszewski

Avery Color Studios
Au Train, Michigan 49806
1991

Library of Congress Card # 90-86206
ISBN # 0-932212-67-0
First Edition March 1991

Front Cover Creation
Photography by Hoyt Avery
Ghost Ship by Edward Pusick

Illustration of the E. M. Ford by
Wesley Mutch

Published
by Avery Color Studios
Au Train, Michigan 49806

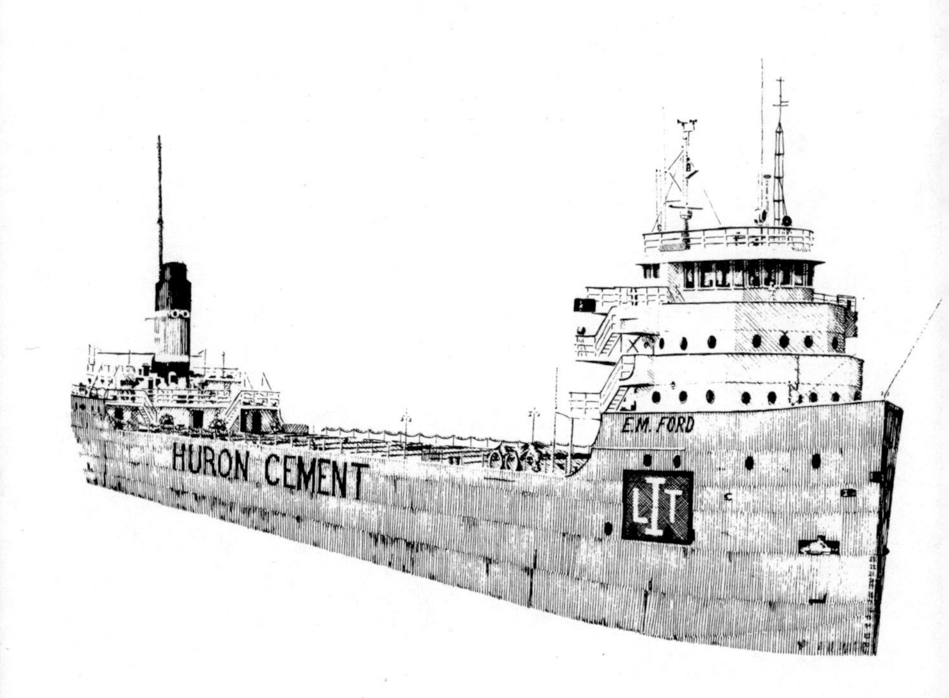

Launched on May 25, 1898 at Lorain, Ohio, the **E. M. Ford** is (as of this writing) the oldest active bulk freighter on the planet. She started her career as the oreboat **Presque Isle,** and appropriately sails right through many of the chapters within this book. This illustration done by Wesley Mutch, of Marquette, Michigan was draw from a photo taken of the **E. M. Ford** by D. J. Story in 1989 and shows her as an elegant tribute to the longevity and determination of those who sail the Great Lakes.

Table of Contents

DEDICATION

To Willie McGarrity, one of my grandpa's.

When I was only three and four years old, my family would rent a cabin on the shores of Lake Huron. Grandpa McGarrity would wake me, long before the others and together we would peer through the picture window, watching the sun rise, the waves lap, and the big oreboats push by. I would give all that I own to have just one of those moments back again.

INTRODUCTION

On the Great Lakes, a ship is a boat, speeds and distances are measured in statute miles instead of knots, and soda pop is just "pop." Kids grow up thinking of every vessel that pushes across the lake's horizon as simply an "oreboat" regardless of its cargo, destination or company. When you use the word oreboat, anyone who lives on or around the Great Lakes knows exactly what you're talking about. It was in the author's youth that a special fascination with the oreboats was seeded. Peering out across the blue lake at a giant oreboat the mind of a child runs wild at the thought of boats gone by, mysterious shipwrecks lying in the depths, and the people who walked their decks. As an adult, one becomes saturated from reading about the same two dozen or so shipwrecks, when hundreds wait in history, their stories untold. And so, in this book the true stories of the lesser known oreboats and the people who walked their decks will be told, to the best of the author's ability. At best some history will be documented, at least some entertaining reading will be provided.

Within this book you will find historical narratives, or true stories. Tales of actual vessels, people and events. In all cases the author has taken great care to present the events as they have happened. The information in the sources used as reference can vary greatly. A case in point being the day and time the steamer William F. Sauber departed Ashland, Wisconsin in 1903. There were six different sources that specifically listed her departure at four different times on two different days. There were three sources, however, that placed the Sauber abeam Manitou Island in Lake Superior at one specific time. Using that single bit of information and an Avstar computer, it was possible to figure the Sauber's speed over the given distance and discover her true time of departure from the variables that were given. A great deal of the same level of research went into all of these tales.

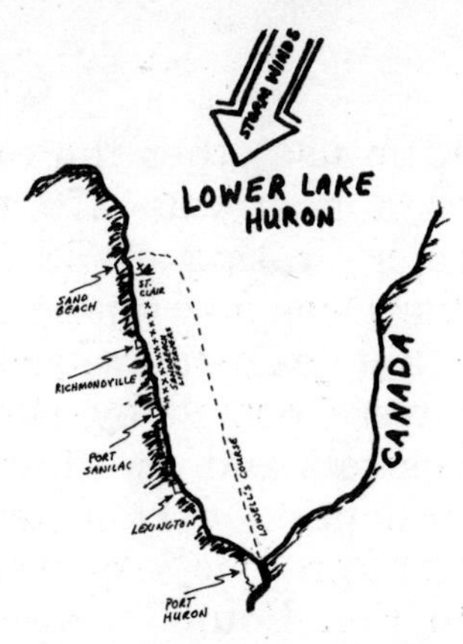

Hard Pullin' For The Sand Beach Lifesavers

On Monday the first day of October, 1888 a strong gray north, northwest storm was blowing across all of the Great Lakes. Being mauled were Lake Huron, Michigan and Erie. A nasty bit of fall weather seemed to be dusting Lake Huron worst of all. Just after noon on that deplorable Monday, the wooden lumber-steamer Lowell pushed upbound out of the St. Clair River and into Lake Huron with a six barge tow. This was the era of powerful wooden steamers; long strings of five or six barges were quite common. Pounding behind the Lowell this afternoon were the wooden consorts Lilly May, Oliver Cromwell, William Young, Sea Gull, Magnet, and last of all the barge St. Clair.

Constructed in 1854, the St. Clair had originally sailed the Lakes as a proud sidewheel steamer. Early in her career a fire gutted the boat and left her with no use other than that of a tow-barge. Her burden now was 270 tons and she carried an Inspector's rating of B2. An estimated value of 3000 dollars was now put on the old boat, a far cry from her value as a sidewheeler. Two-thirds of the St. Clair were owned by Detroit shipping magnate J.W. Westcott and one third of the barge was owned by her captain, C.H. Jones of Bay City, Michigan. Her cargo on this trip was 300 tons of coal consigned to Ben Boutelle, also of Bay City. The coal was being carried at the owner's risk, meaning it was not insured.

Interestingly, the St. Clair was not the only cut-down steamer in the Lowell's tow. Second in tow was the barge Oliver Cromwell, a once graceful propeller forced now into evil days. Having been built at Buffalo in 1858 the Cromwell had sunk to the bottom in the 1860's. After several years the old propeller was raised and cut down to 276 tons burden. Like the St. Clair, the Cromwell carried a rating of B2 was now worth only 3000 dollars. For many years the Cromwell had been consort the the steamer Passiac. In those days she was owned by Captain Blodgett of Detroit; now her services were owned by J. W. Westcott, much the same as the old St. Clair.

As the seven wooden boats pounded upbound into the rapidly darkening afternoon, the storm grew to gale force. Thick wet snow was spit from the low clouds and collected in large white clumps on their hulls. Normally, weather of this kind would give a vessel master cause to turn and run for shelter. The Lowell's problem now was her long tail of six consorts. Turning 180 degrees and running for Port Huron would be the logical choice, but only for a steamer with a great deal of power and without barges to burden her. In the Lowell's favor was the fact that the wind was blowing from nearly due north and her present course took her almost head to the seas. She could press upbound at least to the next natural port of shelter, and her master would be able to further assess the weather in this time. By not turning, he would not risk exposing his consorts to the trough of the seas which could overstress the hawsers and break up the tow.

The next natural port of shelter on the route of the seven storm swept boats was Sand Beach. Known in modern times as Harbor Beach, Michigan, Sand Beach has been a place of shelter from Lake Huron's fury since the beginning of navigation on the Lake. For the Lowell, making the port of Sand Beach would mean sailing into the storm until just after dark, but once there she would only have to turn 90 degrees and would only have to pull her consorts along the trough of the seas instead of out of the trough. The steamer would then be able to gain shelter while exposing her tow to a minimum of stress.

While the decision to keep the Lowell and her Bay City bound consort St. Clair pushing up toward Sand Beach was being made, another Bay City boat was fighting for life on Lake Michigan. The propeller George T. Hope downbound light to Chicago for a cargo of 3.25 cent corn was towing the schooner-barge Baker. After loading, the Hope would head to Buffalo, but Lake Michigan had other ideas. Winds of hurricane force blasted snow across the two boats. The Hope, which was constructed at the Davidson Shipyard in Bay City, was a strong wooden vessel and Captain Fick was an able master. As the pair passed Milwaukee, the Hope cast the Baker loose, the barge's cargo was consigned to that port and a powerful tug was now on the way out to meet her. Continuing on her way, the Hope sailed alone into the deep black evening. At nine o'clock p.m., a loud crack resounded aft below decks. The steamer slid into the trough and broached too. Her wheelsman attempted to turn the boat in accordance with Captain Fick's orders, but the wheel spun useless in his hands...the Hope's rudder chains had parted. Soon the sails that were used to augment the boat's steam engine were blasted to shreds by the wind. Her water casks were lifted from their racks and swept overboard. A repair gang was quickly mustered aft and a temporary tiller was rigged to replace the boat's broken steering equipment. It took eight of her crew above decks and four more crouched between decks to work the rig. After nearly a half hour of sweating and swearing the steamer was brought around head to the seas. Now upbound the Hope was attempting to run for the safety of Milwaukee Harbor. It took eight and one half hours for the crippled boat to get back.

The Hope's corn cargo was reconsigned the next day to the Susan E. Peck at a substantially reduced profit. Captain Fick had lost a profitable cargo, but he had escaped the rampaging gale with his boat relatively intact. Just after dinner on Lake Huron, Sailors Lorne Fertaw of Bay City, George McFarlane of Cleveland, and Henry Anderson of Australia were in the St. Clair's snug galley reassuring Cook Julia Greawreath of Sebwaing, Michigan, that the old St. Clair was well able to withstand this storm. Julia was highly favored aboard the St. Clair and each crew member sheltered her as an adolescent boy protects a baby sister. Besides, as Seaman Fertaw calmly informed her while munching on a crisp apple, the St. Clair, while in this loaded condition, was faring much better than a boat such as the Cromwell, which was empty and riding high out of the water. All the sailors reasoned that the Lowell would have to put into Sand Beach to wait for weather.

Everywhere around the Lakes wooden boats ran for ports of refuge. The Port of Alpena with the natural shelter of Thunder Bay quickly became the gathering place for the storm pounded vessels on northern Lake Huron. In lee of Thunder Bay Island the propeller Susguehanna dropped her anchors. She had worked her way north from Point Aux Barques into the building storm with her rudder chains parted. Her crew had quickly rigged a tiller and operated the rudder by hand all the way up the Lake. Also in lee of the island, the steamer Townsend and her consort were anchored. The steamers Loomis, Gettysburg, and Ira Brown were also tucked snugly below the island's shelter. From the Presque Isle coast the schooner Ayer ran for cover, she also dropped her hooks below Thunder Bay Island. Struggling into the tempest that fitful Monday, the propeller Wilson approached with the barges Dan Rogers, F. B. Gardner, Manitowoc, and Chester B. Jones in tow. All were loaded with lumber and were being savagely mauled by the angry Lake. The Wilson was taking the worst of the beating. By the time the Wilson and her string of barges reached Thunder Bay the steamer's masts had been broken down and she was wallowing sluggishly in the heavy sea. Onboard the Rogers they saw the Wilson's towing hawser go slack. The steamer was abandoning her consorts within reach of Thunder Bay's shelter. Each barge raised the meager sails that they carried for just this kind of situation. Under sail, each barge would now at least have a fighting chance of reaching safety. As the crew of the Rogers worked to raise her sail they saw the Wilson pounding north into the Lake and storm. Suddenly her lights vanished into the darkness.

Each of the Wilson's barges succeeded in making their way into Thunder Bay. All were badly waterlogged, but the barge Gardner was the worst off, while rounding Thunder Bay Island she fell off into the trough of the sea and sprang a leak. Now unmanageable the old schooner had her sails torn away from her mainmast and her foremast came crashing down as her booms and gaffs were carried away. From Alpena, the lifesavers rowed their surfboat out to the Gardner whose entire deckload was now being plucked away by the Lake. At the same time the tug Ralph and the propeller Garden City were steaming out to rescue the drifting barges. All of the Wilson's tow were rounded up and brought safely into Alpena. Once there the crew of the Rogers stated flatly that they had seen the steamer Wilson go down with all hands.

In southern Lake Huron the St. Clair and the other boats in the Lowell's tow were coming abeam of Sand Beach near the tip of Michigan's thumb. The steamer hauled to port and her long string of barges arced around in a giant semi-circle. A sharp crest of bitter cold water rose up to smack the steamer Lowell on her beam, another wave followed, and then another. Quickly the Lowell was driven south of the harbor entrance. If she kept on, both the steamer and her consorts would be driven aground. The wind and seas made it impossible for Lowell to successfully turn in either direction. There would be no way she could pull her consorts out of the trough of the seas. A quick, desperate move had to be made if any of the seven boats were to survive. There was no choice for the Lowell but to drop her barges.

Suddenly like six leaves on a windblown pond the barges began to be blown south. The St. Clair drifted for a short distance, just long enough to cut herself free from the barge Magnet which was ahead of her. Both anchors of the St. Clair were put over and dragged in the sandy bottom for a time before taking a firm hold. Three quarters of a mile off shore, the St. Clair sat being beaten constantly by the Lake. The other barges came to anchor one by one until all six were head to the seas.

At the Sand Beach lifesaving station Captain Plough had been watching the amber lamps of the seven boats with a great deal of interest. The snow squalls blotted out the long string of boats from time to time, now it had become clear that something was very wrong. At six p.m. the lifesavers launched their surfboat with the intent of helping the Lowell reconstruct her tow. The Lowell however had other plans. Instead of turning back into the open lake and gathering her abandoned barges, the steamer ran for the shelter of the inner harbor. Pulling to the Lilly May the lifesavers sheltered their tiny surfboat beneath the barge's stern. With a good deal of amazement they watched as the lights of the Lowell swung smoothly into the Sand Beach harbor blending with the lamps and masts of a dozen other boats. After about an hour the lifesavers pulled from the Lilly May, which was riding very well in the storm, and headed for the old St. Clair who appeared to be taking the worst of it. Upon arriving at the St. Clair's side the lifesavers urged her crew to leave their boat and come with them to safety. The barge's crew to the last person refused to leave their boat. Departing the St. Clair the lifesavers began the hard pull back toward Sand Beach harbor. On any sunny mid-summer day rowing a surfboat from where the St. Clair was now anchored to Sand Beach was quite a chore. Tonight a frozen gale-force wind was raising up mountainous waves that slammed over the boat and blasting cold, wet snow over her people. Returning to Sand Beach would be much harder pulling than going out to the St. Clair.

As the lifesavers were struggling back toward the harbor,Sailor Maurice McKenna went below to look over the St. Clair's cargo of coal. His breath created small puffs of steam that were illuminated by his oil lantern as he made his way down into the blackness of the hold. It was much more like a giant old wooden walk-in icebox than a boat full of coal. The pounding of the Lake drowned out any sound that would have indicated what was going on deep in that hold. McKenna was surprised to find a great deal of water sloshing among the coal cargo. Moments later his surprise turned to shock as his lamp shined upon the barge's aged wooden hull. Giant streams of lake water were gushing from nearly every seam. The St. Clair was going to pieces beneath his feet as the lifesavers were rowing back to Sand Beach.

While the St. Clair was being pounded by Lake Huron, the crew of another cut-down side wheeler were on their way to Chicago with nothing but the wet clothes on their backs. They were the men of the barge R.M. Rice which had been ripped to pieces Sunday morning on Lake Michigan. Constructed at Detroit in 1866, the Rice was at that time the fastest and proudest sidewheel steamer on the Lakes. Along with the steamer

Morning Star, the Rice formed the beginnings of the Detroit and Cleveland Line. In 1876, the Rice was lying at Detroit when she caught fire. So extensive was the fire damage that like the Cromwell and St. Clair the only use for the Rice after that was as a lumber barge. Her owner on this rude Sunday morning in 1888 was Patrick O'Day of Buffalo.

In tow of the steamer Huron City and fully loaded with a cargo of lumber, the Rice had been beaten to death by the merciless seas. Captain Stedman had tried to signal the Huron City to take his leaking barge to Grand Haven, Michigan, but the steamer simply cast the Rice adrift far north of that port. The crew of the old barge had already been at the creaking hand pumps for several hours, but now with giant seas smashing over the old barge it was impossible to man her pumps. Taking to the lifeboats, the crew of the Rice abandoned their boat 20 miles north of Grand Haven. Moments later the R.N. Rice went to pieces and sank to Lake Michigan's bottom. For three frigid hours, the shipwrecked crew drifted on an enraged Lake Michigan. Finally the steamer Huron City came back into view, and after a distress signal was raised from the lifeboat, the sailors were picked up.

Back at Sand Beach, the lifesavers reached shore and landed their surfboat. After only one half of an hour on dry land they spotted a distress lantern being waved from the St. Clair. Another hard pull took the nine lifesavers out to the old barge and at eleven o'clock p.m. the seven crewmembers were taken off the old barge. With 16 persons in the surfboat it would now be impossible to row back to Sand Beach against the wind and waves. Captain Plough elected wisely to run before the storm and try to make Port Sanilac 23 miles to the south. Off they rowed into wind and seas of that stormy night.

Before midnight, the anchors of the barges Magnet and Seagull began to drag as the storm pushed both boats toward shallow water. One after another the two barges pulled up their hooks and put out their small sails, turned with the wind and limped into the blackness toward Port Huron. From Sand Beach harbor scores of vesselmen watched as the lights of the two barges swung about and vanished into the storm. The chances of either of the two old wooden barges making the safety of Port Huron through the maelstrom of wind and waves were remote at best.

Through the long dark hours before dawn on Tuesday, October 2, 1888, a tiny wooden surfboat crammed with the nine lifesavers and the seven crewmembers of the barge St. Clair pulled their way toward Port Sanilac. Giant crests of ice water slapped down on the small vessel constantly filling it. Shivering uncontrollably, the eight men manning the oars pulled for all they were worth. This was a storm that had beaten to death giant wooden lakeboats, and here were 16 poor souls in a small surfboat deep in its clutches. In the darkness the men in the surfboat saw that Julia Greawreath was near death of hypothermia. Gallantly they removed their heavy jackets and wrapped the wool clothing tightly around her.

Daylight on Lake Huron revealed the barge St. Clair being driven into shallow water and quickly going to pieces just south of Sand Beach. The Oliver Cromwell, also of the Lowell's tow, was driven ashore but was holding together. Riding safely at anchor outside of Sand Beach, the Lilly May and William Young waited for the Lowell to return for them. Aside from the Lowell's wayward consorts, the schooner Racine had run into problems south of Sand Beach. Having gotten the better of the schooner, the storm pushed her ashore. During the storm the propeller Edwards and her two barges had made the shelter of Sand Beach. Also tucked snugly inside of Sand Beach harbor were the propeller Germanin and four barges, the Alpena and her consort, the Annie Smith and her barge, plus the vessels Point Abieo, Bessie, William Chislolm, Ruby Montana, H. C.Winslow and Nyack. The tugs Bob Anderson and Champion were sheltered among the other lakeboats. At East Tawas, daylight revealed the steamers Metropolis, D. F. Rose and Sakie Shepherd along with the barges Boscobel, Agnes, A. Gebhart and Buckeye State along with 14 other vessels in shelter.

South of Sand Beach, at the village of Richmondville, the steambarge Mattawan had been driven into shallow water and was aground being beaten by the Lake. The Mattawan out of Montreal had the barge Gibraltar, of St. Catherines in tow. Before the steamer went aground the barge was cut loose, but crashed ashore three miles south. The Mattawan was now flying distress signals and appeared about to go to pieces in the surf. Near the Mattawan's wreck sight was the home of the Allen brothers of Richmondville. Spotting the steamer's distress signals the two brothers loaded their tiny rowboat into a small horsedrawn wagon and trucked it down the beach to a point opposite the stranded steamer. A small group of friends and neighbors of the brothers were gathered on the beach where the two intended to launch their small boat. Despite the protests of friends and neighbors regarding the safety of the brothers, the Allens launched their boat into the storm-churned lake. Soon the brothers reached the steamer and offered to take members of her crew to shore. Most of the Mattawan's crew scoffed at the notion of running through the rampaging waves in a tiny rowboat, but two men decided it was worth the risk and climbed in. After three-quarters of a mile of wet rowing the Allen brothers landed their rowboat and discharged their two shipwrecked sailors. Relaunching their boat the brothers headed out a second time. Onboard the stranded steamer her captain had been encouraged by the success of the Allens and ordered the boat's yawl launched. The very first sailor who stepped into the steamer's yawl was immediately tossed out into the Lake and had to swim for shore. Ten minutes later he clawed his way onto the beach nearly dead from exposure. Six other crewmen did reach shore in the yawl plus another two picked up by the heroic Allen brothers on their second trip. The action of the Allens did not surprise local residents, after all it was the same two men who in 1885 rescued the crew of the steamer Havana.

As the crew of the Mattawan were being rescued, the drenched lifesavers from Sand beach along with seven shipwrecked crewmembers of the St. Clair were approaching Port Sanilac. It had been a rough passage, shortly after leaving the St. Clair the surfboat's rudder had been plucked away and they were forced to use the oars for steering. The final problem for the lifesavers would be getting under the lee of the dock at Port Sanilac. Once in the dock's shelter the surf boat could be landed easily. As the surfboat rounded the dock it fell into the trough of the seas and a sudden, quick breaker struck the boat on her beam rolling her twice over and tossing all sixteen people into the ice water.

Ironically, Ship's Cook Julia Greawreath was the first to perish. The bundles of spare clothing that the men had wrapped around her to keep her warm now quickly weighed her down; she sank immediately to the bottom of Lake Huron. Captain C.H. Jones, Henry Anderson, George McFarlane, and Lorne Fertaw also did not reach shore alive. Only Maurice McKenna and John Rose were able to survive the swim to dry land. Of the lifesavers, all survived, their heroic effort however was spoiled by the ferocious lake. On the windswept beach at Port Sanilac the Sand Beach lifesavers sat exhausted. Lake Huron had thwarted them 100 feet from victory, it had been a hard pull from Sand Beach.

Late on that second day of October, 1888 three lost lakeboats came back from the dead. At Port Huron the *Lowell's* barges *Sea Gull* and *Magnet* limped into the sky-blue St. Clair River. Once within the safety of Port Huron, the *Magnet* slowly sank. Meanwhile up at Alpena the steamer *Wilson*, that the crew of the *Dan Rogers* swore they had all seen go down with all hands, staggered into port. She had run north for Presque Isle Harbor, but was beaten back by the storm a few miles short of safety. Apparently when the men of the *Rogers* saw the *Wilson's* light vanish, a snow squall had come between the two boats giving the illusion that the steamer had foundered suddenly. Steaming past the startled crew of the *Rogers*, the badly damaged *Wilson* must have seemed like a ghost ship, but she was really just another battered boat that had to pull hard to survive.

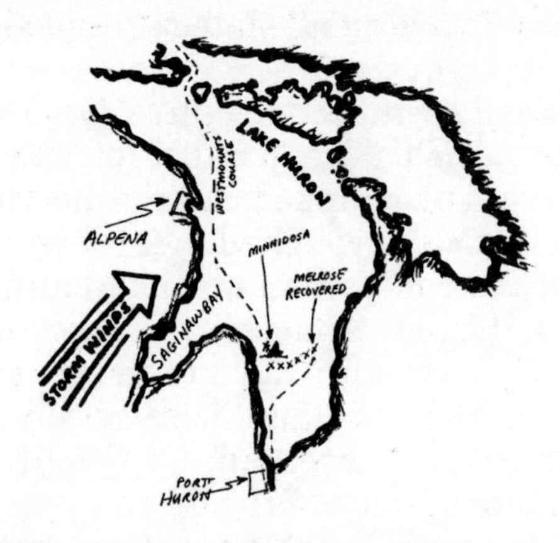

Where Is The Minnedosa?

When looking back across Great Lakes history, it is rare that any accounts of storm-pounded boats seeking shelter in Saginaw Bay or the river that flows into it are found. The reason for this is that in any kind of storm from any direction the very worst place to be is anywhere on, or near Saginaw Bay. The Bay is 30 miles wide, over 55 miles long, and very shallow. As a result, any kind of storm will kick up big sharp waves very quickly. Also, the bay angles out into Lake Huron in what seems to be just the right direction to deal punishment to boats which are simply passing by its mouth. In some cases, the Saginaw Bay has delvered mortal punishment to a vessel only to release it to the big Lake to be claimed hours later.

October of 1905 had been a cold, storm raked month on the Great Lakes. The fall storms had arrived early this year and the boats and their crews did exactly what they had always done about the weather; they just worked in it. On the north shores of Lake Superior, in the port of Fort William, three boats were loading wheat. It was pre-dawn on Wednesday, October 18th. The rates were high and the annual fall grain rush was in full swing. It was the objective of all the grain carriers to haul as much wheat as possible before the thick winter ice locked tight the navigation channels. Bearing this in mind the steel steamer Westmount, and the old wooden schooner-barges Minnedosa and Melrose topped off their standard loads. Each barge captain and the first mate of the Westmount had in turn also taken on a substantial overload of wheat. In her loading, the Minnedosa took on 60,000 bushels of fresh Canadian wheat. Her wooden hull groaned and creaked as the full load sank it down to the 14 foot mark, maximum draft for the boat's transit of the old Welland Canal. Then, through the swirl of grain dust, the schooner-barge's captain, Jack Phillips, gave the order to load another 15,000 bushels. Her total burden would now be 75,000 bushels and her draft would not allow the boat through the canal. She would be forced to off-load the extra tonnage at the head of the canal and ship it by rail to the Lake Ontario side where she could take it back aboard for the rest of the trip. It would be an extra expense, but the price of grain was high enough to justify this.

Under the cold amber glow of oil lamps mounted on both the dock and boats, the lines were cast off. The Westmount's whistle echoed one long blast as she pulled her consort toward the open lake on a short hawser. Following the steamer faithfully, came first the Minnedosa and finally the tired old

Melrose. As the three entered Lake Superior the tow lines were let out several hundred feet. A modest October storm was blowing right from the start, and both schooners began to creak and moan loudly. The passage to the Soo would not be pleasant.

The concept of schooner-barges was unique to the Great Lakes. Small lumber carrying schooners such as the Melrose had operated with great efficiency for most of the middle 1800's. Then the appearance of the big lake steamboat quickly outdated these freshwater wind-grabbers. Rather than abandoning the hundreds of wooden sailing boats, the vessel owners found that by removing the sails and rigging they could tow as many as six of these wooden hulls behind one of their steamers and increase their cargo carried per trip substantially. So popular became this concept that boats such as the Minnedosa were being built as schooners with little or no intent of ever having them move under sail. When the Minnedosa was launched in 1890, she was among more than a score of big wooden schooners that would never see wind-power.

On this October morning, the 245 foot Minnedosa found herself bound by both ends to a pair of her sister ships. Her 1315 ton wooden hull was being dragged helplessly across the violent surface of Lake Superior. At mid-day there came wind-whipped snow flurries. It was that late October snow that doesn't accumulate, but spatters against the deck houses and then vanishes into the lake. Aft in his quarters, Captain Phillips kept a close watch on his boat.

The good captain was also paying special attention to his guest for this trip. From Kingston,

Ontario, his wife had come to join him. Despite the most reassuring words of the Minnedosa's crew and captain, it was obvious that Mrs. Phillips was not going to have a very enjoyable trip down the Lakes.

The wind was blowing fresh from the northeast and Lake Superior's waves were pounding all three boats nearly at their beams. A constant rolling pained the soaked wooden hulls, yet all three crews considered this to be just another of Superior's fall storms. They went about their duties amid the flapping tarpaulins and squeaking rigging as best they could. Everyone knew that soon they would pass from Lake Superior's temper and into Lake Huron's less furious company. Being the property of the Montreal Transportation Company, all three boats were well acquainted with the moods of upper Lakes. The 267 ton Melrose having more experience than the others. Constructed in 1852 at Three Mile Bay, the old schooner was a true veteran of Great Lakes wind and wave. On the other hand, the 255 foot Westmount had slid down the ways at the Swan, Hunter yard in Newcastle-On-Tyne, England in 1903 and was a newcomer to the Lakes.

Just before dawn on Thursday, the 19th of October the Minnedosa, along with her fellow boats Melrose and Westmount, slipped quietly past Ile Parisienne in Whitefish Bay. All three crews busied themselves at the task of shortening the towing hawsers in preparation for locking down at the Soo. At about this same time, the doomed boat Kaliyuga was clearing the locks down-bound. Like the trio of boats in Whitefish Bay, the Kaliyuga was being lulled by the relative calm of the protected waters of the St. Mary's river, yet before this day would end, the Kaliyuga and her 14 crewmembers would vanish without a trace on an angry Lake Huron. The storm brewing to the west was not about to warn its potential victims of its true fury.

It was mid-morning by the time the steamer Westmount pulled the Minnedosa and Melrose clear of the locks. Captain Alex Milligan of the Westmount peered intently through the pilot house windows as his boat and her consorts rounded Mission Point. The weather really wasn't looking much better. Over the hills on the Canadian side the sky was a deep gray and the treeline seemed to vanish in and out of the clouds. To the west over the locks, it looked just as bad with the gray clouds reaching down as if to swallow the Soo itself. Tapping his barometer, Captain Milligan kept in mind that the weather at the Soo would often be nearly this bad in late August, so for late October, it was the rule rather than the exception. He guided the trio slowly onward down the St. Mary's river, often reaching for the boat's big brass whistle-pull to hoot passing signals to the multitude of upbound vessels.

At dinner time aboard the creaking old Melrose, Captain R.A. Davey was mustering his crew in preparation for their downbound passage to Port Huron. This 30 year veteran of Great Lakes sailing looked ahead as the two lead boats, Minnedosa and Westmount, passed Detour and pounded on into Lake Huron. Should the weather worsen, it was Captain Davey who would have the most to worry about. His boat was not only the smallest, but also the oldest of the trio. And like the others, the Melrose was overloaded.

Darkness came early, and no sooner had the lights of Detour vanished over the horizon than the storm began to quickly intensify. The wind, still from the northeast, now howled at 40 miles an hour with gusts over 50. Now the snow became thick bursts of cold pellets that sting a man's skin as if shot from a sandblaster. Lake Huron's waves rose to become giant mountains of heaving frigid liquid. Each boat was repeatedly lifted to the crest of the seas by their stern only to plunge again and again down the back side of the wave and into the trough. It was clear that Lake Huron would not be better company than Superior. The two wooden consorts groaned and leaked as if each moment would be their last. Something would have to give if the two wooden boats were to survive the night.

When the trio was just north of Adams Point on the Michigan coast, the "give" happened. The wind shifted suddenly from north, northeast to west, northwest. Captain Milligan of the Westmount could now run for the lee of the Michigan shore. There, he and his consorts could sail in comparatively protected waters.

Onboard the Westmount, mate John Black looked back to check on the condition of the schooners being towed aft. Even though both boats were still taking quite a dusting by the off-shore wind and waves, neither was showing any kind of distress signal. He could clearly see the amber lamps of the Minnedosa rocking between the snow squalls. Far behind, he could also make out the dull glow of the Melrose's oil lamps. She, too, appeared to be working well in the seas.

Curving southward, the three grain laden boats hugged the Michigan shore. The wind-whipped snow grew stronger and the boats found themselves isolated from one another by bursts of blinding snow. Captain Phillips, onboard the Minnedosa, had soon lost sight of the other two boats. All that could be seen was a long steel towline stretching forward into the darkness toward the Westmount and a long thick rope hawser stretching behind where the Melrose was following. Captain Phillips knew as well as all the rest of the crews that in order to get to Port Huron, the trio would soon have to leave the safety of Michigan's shoreline and cut across the mouth of Saginaw Bay. Once past the tip of Michigan's thumb, they could again run in the lee of land. The problem was the Bay, which even in 1905, was littered with the bones of nearly 30 proud lakeboats. Now, the worst storm in recent history was churning up Lake Huron and Saginaw Bay. The three overloaded grain carriers would have to challenge the Bay if they were to survive. They pressed on through a dark gray Friday.

Just south of Oscoda, the Westmount turned to a heading of nearly due east to bring the three boats across Saginaw Bay. The storm was producing big sharp combers on the bay. They were striking the boats from behind and came in rapid succession. The hammering was incredible and the two wooden boats began to spring and leak. When the trio was halfway across the bay, the storm reached its peak. Near hurricane force winds tortured the Westmount, Minnedosa, and Melrose. Giant cascades of ice water slammed over the rails of each boat, bursting in doorways, smashing out windows and blasting through the wooden seams of the two old schooners as if sprayed from a fire hose.

The Minnedosa was being ravaged by the merciless Saginaw Bay. Her timbers were being bent and sprung from their normal positions on her hull and each wave now began to flood the old wooden boat. She had carried an overload of 15,000 bushels before, but never in near hurricane force winds. Now this extra weight was just what Saginaw Bay needed to aid it in pounding the boat to pieces. By the time the three grain boats escaped Saginaw Bay's brutal clutches, the Minnedosa had been mortally wounded. To her captain and crew it was not a question of if she would founder, but when. Since there was no way of communicating between vessels in that pitch black of Saturday morning, October 21, 1905, the individual vessel masters could only guess what condition the other boats were in. The Minnedosa was clearly about to sink, and Captain Phillips could only assume that the older and smaller Melrose, which was tied to the Minnedosa's stern, was in the same or perhaps worse condition. When the Minnedosa sinks, she will take the Melrose with her.

In the pilothouse of the steamer Westmount, Captain Milligan was equally unaware of the status of the two wooden boats he was pulling behind. He knew that both boats had taken quite a beating coming across the bay, but was given no indication that either of the consorts was on the brink of death. Even as the three boats were rounding the thumb, the storm was still working them quite badly. Looking aft from the Westmount's pilothouse, Captain Milligan could see the Minnedosa's lamps between snow squalls and at times he could also see the lamps of the old Melrose, but in the sackcloth darkness, it was impossible to discern their condition. He had no reason to believe that either boat was in any kind of distress.

Eight miles off of Harbor Beach, the Minnedosa met her fate. Her seams and planking split open with the roar of inrushing lake water. The boat groaned and began to grow suddenly sluggish. Captain Phillips knew that only seconds remained before his boat would plunge to the bottom, taking the Melrose with her. Above the clamor of the dying vessel, Captain Phillips ordered a crewman to grab an ax and meet him aft. Once there, he then ordered the deckhand to cut the thick rope hawser that bound the old Melrose to the Minnedosa. Again and again the burly crewman lifted the ax above his head and chopped down on the towline. It began to fray and then with a resounding cannon-like "crack", the Melrose was cut free.

Moments later on the Westmount, the pilothouse watch felt a tremor and then were jerked forward, almost off their feet, as if the boat had struck something. Mate John Black peered aft through the pilot house windows to see what was the matter. The lamps of the old Melrose were far off in the distance, drifting several points to port. To his utter shock, the Minnedosa's lights were gone. Mate Black scanned the raging seas, perhaps a snow squall had blotted out her lights. The big schooner was just plain gone. "My God, Captain," the mate shouted, "where is the Minnedosa?!"

The word spread in seconds through the Westmount, and soon all available hands were on the stern rail peering silently aft as waves of ice water burst over the boat soaking the group of them. The steel towing hawser was stretched almost straight down into the heaving lake. Captain Milligan looked up through the ice cold spray and could barely see a single lamp from the drifting Melrose far off to port. There was the very real possibility that she would go down soon, or even be cut-down in the blackness by another freighter. And here sat the, Westmount anchored to the dead Minnedosa thirty fathoms below.

Rescue of the Melrose was now Captain Milligan's duty. He ordered the Westmount's windless turned, taking up the steel towline. With a lurch, the towpost of the Minnedosa was ripped from her wooden deck. The remains of the post were hoisted to the aft rail of the Westmount and the steamer headed out into the open lake to rescue the helpless Melrose. It was just before 1:00 a.m.

Turning the Westmount was no easy task in this kind of weather. The storm was still near its peak and the waves towered nearly as high as the steamer's tall smoke-stack. Sliding into the trough of the sea, the grain laden boat would now need every ounce of power she could muster to pull herself out. Captain Milligan rang full ahead on the pilothouse chadburn. Down in the engine room, it was a hellish sight. The boat's black gang shoveled for all they were worth. Slinging a number three coal scoop was no simple matter and when the deck under your feet is pitching at angles as great as 35 degrees the task is nearly impossible. The fire hold crew shoveled on. Each scoop of coal was greeted by a spit of fire and a lash of searing heat. They were not stoking for their own lives, but for the lives of those onboard the helpless Melrose.

The Westmount rolled insanely. Thick black smokepoured from her stack and spread across an angry Lake Huron. Captain Milligan could not see the old Melrose, but knew instinctively what direction she was in. He also knew instinctively that if he did not reach the schooner and get a line aboard her, she would be blown out into the open lake. There, the small wooden boat would soon be pounded to death. This was now a race against time and a raging lake that was not satisfied with the victim that Saginaw Bay had fed it less than an hour ago. Captain Milligan ordered the Westmount's wheel swung to port. The steel steamer pitched nose down as a giant roller lifted her stern. She slid nearly sideways down the other side of the big wave. The big boat mushed at the stern and shuddered. Neatly stowed sailor's possessions were tossed helter-skelter about the crew quarters. A second mountain of ice water slammed against the Westmount's side, rolling her on her beam-ends and washing her decks. Billows of black coal smoke engulfed the rolling steamer. Pausing for a moment, the Westmount gained momentum and began to make headway. Captain Milligan had succeeded in turning his boat toward the Melrose.

Lake Huron had pounded the relatively young Minnedosa to its sandy bottom and as far as Captain Milligan could figure the older and smaller Melrose would go at any moment. In fact, she may already have been swallowed by the hungry cold lake. It was nearly a half hour before a single amber oil lamp could be seen pitching dimly in the distance. The light vanished as each wave rose up between the two boats. Every time the tiny lamp disappeared, the crew of the Westmount would hold their breath in unison, fearing that the Melrose had plunged to the bottom before their eyes. The ultimate disappointment would be to reach the battered Melrose, yet be too late to save her. Suddenly, the dim lamp vanished and this time did not re-appear at its regular interval. The pilothouse crew pressed toward the windows wiping the condensation away in order to get a better view. A giant wave smacked the Westmount's stern, rolled along her deck and plowed into the rear of her pilothouse. Through the frigid spray, the pilothouse crew peered for what seemed to be hours, but was only minutes. The thick snow squall that had suddenly come between the two boats now cleared as quickly as it had arrived. The lights of the old Melrose re-appeared.

Captain Milligan drew his boat as close as he dared to the rolling Melrose. For an hour and a half, the crew of the Westmount worked in the freezing spray and blowing snow in an attempt to get a line aboard the thrashing schoonerbarge. Each time, their efforts were thwarted by the darkness and the cold of the wind and waves. Captain Milligan decided that his efforts would be more fruitful in the daylight. He pulled the Westmount a safe distance from the Melrose to wait the five hours until daylight.

For nearly an hour, the two boats tossed and drifted in the blackness of the storm. There was still no telling the condition of the Melrose. The storm surrounding the two boats had been too dark and too wild for the Westmount's crew to communicate with the crew of the Melrose. Captain Milligan could only drift in the shrieking wind and hope that the tossing lights of the old Melrose did not vanish in front of him. At about 4:00 a.m., Captain Milligan had convinced himself that the old schooner-barge had only a short time left on top of the water. The Westmount had to not only try again, but this time succeed in capturing the Melrose.

Once more, the waves battered the two boats and the wind shrieked darkness hindered the rescue. For an hour the two crews worked. Finally at 5:00 a.m., a line was made fast between the two boats. The Melrose had drifted over twenty miles, more than halfway to Canada. Now all that the two boats had to do was survive the run to the lee of the Michigan shore. There was the strong possibility that the Westmount may find herself anchored to another dead schooner-barge before reaching Sarnia.

Daylight found the Westmount and Melrose pushing their way into the St. Clair river. Captain Milligan made dock in Sarnia and for the first time since leaving the Soo was able to speak to Captain Davey of the Melrose. There in the shelter of the river the vessel masters spoke of the storm behind them, the trip ahead, and the fate of the Minnedosa. Over their shoulder Lake Huron continued to rage in her tantrum. She was a striking beautiful lady without remorse at having claimed another boat and its crew.

A common sight along the walls of all the Great Lakes locks, the four masted schooner barge **Minnedosa** was unique in many respects. One stood out most prominently, the vessel never ran under sail but spent her entire career pulled by a steamer.
Courtesy of Milwaukee Public Library

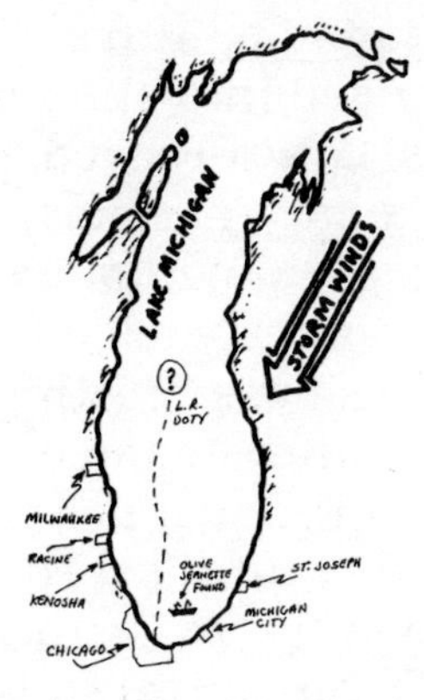

The First Of The Doomed Sisters

The first snow of the winter of 1898 came with the predawn hours of Tuesday, October 25. A storm front stretching as far south as the Gulf of Mexico pushed its way across the Great Lakes and without warning grew in intensity until by Tuesday morning a full gale was blowing. The worst storm in 25 years dumped thick wet snow across all of the Great Lakes. At Sheboygan, Wisconsin, a large group of townsfolk braved the weather to watch Lake Michigan's waves destroy over 100 feet of the Taylor dock. Cresting at nearly 12 feet, the ice cold breaking waves were rolling down from the northeast pushed by a north wind of over 70 miles per hour.

Around the Great Lakes battered vessels hauled for shelter. Wallowing into Alpena came the Union Steamboat Company's powerful 340 foot steel freighter Ramapo. Rarely had this giant steamer been pounded into running from an angry lake, but on this storm-racked night the waves beating on the Ramapo's rudder had caused her steering chains to part. Without the service of her rudder the big boat quickly fell off into the trough of the sea. The mountainous cresting waves began to take advantage of the steamer. Breaking in her cabins and washing through her galley, the icy lake carried away all the boat's provisions. Soon the Ramapo's crew rigged relieving tackles to the boat's rudder arm and the battered steamer ran for Alpena. Once there she joined a tiny fleet of boats sheltering there. The schooners Demond, Hattie, William P. Fessenden, and the steamer Colonial were all waiting out the storm in Alpena's sheltered waters. It was another story for the steel steamer Republic, that challenged Lake Huron's fury only to be thrown onto North Point like a hunk of driftwood.

At the Soo, the 432 foot steel steamer Sir Henry Bessemer hissed into the locks towing the 376 foot whaleback barge Alexander Holley. Both boats were downbound with bellies full of Marquette ore when they were overtaken by the storm. Rain turned quickly into ice pellets and the wind screamed down upon the two boats at nearly 65 miles per hour. With a resounding crack, the steel towline parted and the two boats drifted apart. The Bessemer made nine efforts to pick up the wayward pigboat during the frothing night. Finally the decision was made to stand by the barge until dawn on Tuesday morning. With the aid of dawn's light, a line was made fast between the two boats and they hauled for the Soo.

For nearly four days, from late Sunday night until early Thursday, the storm churned Lake

Michigan. As early as Tuesday afternoon shipping had become a tangled mess. At Michigan City, the wooden steamer H.A. Tuttle laden with grain suddenly broke in half in the mouth of the river. She sat there for 20 hours with giant seas exploding over her broken hull before the lifesavers could remove her crew. The consort to the Tuttle, the 211 foot Aberdeen, was cut loose on the open lake before the steamer failed. Having been constructed at Bay City's Davidson yard in 1892 the Aberdeen was relatively new. Hopefully she could hold her own against the storm. The schooner was last seen adrift on the raging open lake. Both boats were under control of the Minch Transit Company.

Milwaukee's harbor saw a sudden rush of storm-ravaged boats seeking shelter. Out of the maelstrom steamed the Gogebic, dropping both hooks in the harbor's protected waters. Missing was the Gogebic's consort, the wooden schooner barge Pewabic. The might of the storm had forced the steamer to drop her barge out on the open lake so that the Gogebic could turn and run for Milwaukee. The battered schooner was left to her own ends and was last seen drifting near Sheboygan. Running for shelter came the schooner Mabel Wilson, but a giant cresting wave stuck her short of safety and slammed the boat into the breakwater. Luckily for the windgrabber the lake delivered only a glancing blow, and the wounded schooner limped into calm waters. The schooner Barbarian who had dropped her hooks in the bay off Milwaukee during the night was suffering damage at her stern, but seemed to be riding well. Out on the open lake off Racine, Wisconsin the 161 foot schooner D.L. Filer was sighted adrift with her sails blown out and masts down. The Racine Lifesavers aided by the tug Dixon, beat their way out to the drifting schooner and successfully removed her crew.

Port Huron became the safe haven for vessels smart enough not to challenge a roaring Lake Huron. Returning to the shelter of the St. Clair River came the tug Torrent, followed by the steel steamer Niagara. The Mercer, Sweepstakes, Douglas, John Oades, Havana, Stephenson, Coriliss and Centurion all put out lines at Port Huron. The boats coming in off the tossing lake joined a crowd of vessels who were already tucked snugly in the bright blue river. Among the fleet squatting out the storm were the steamers Pontiac, Saginaw, Newaygo, Choctaw, W.D. Rees, Norton, Fayette Brown, Lagonda, Kearsarge, Crescent City, and Onoko. Also sheltering at Port Huron was the Presque Isle, John Duncan, India, Conemaugh, Charlie Crawford. Rounding out Port Huron's roll-call of sheltered boats were the Boston, Arabian, Laura Wesley, Wade, Shenandoah, Crete, and Hadley. Near the height of the storm the crews of all the sheltered boats were quite astonished to see the steamer Bangor steam passively upbound into the wild lake. Her master looking back at the protected fleet gave a deep "harumph," and mumbled, "lose a day because of a little weather...not by a damn sight."

Late into Wednesday night the wind howled and the snow and sleet blew horizontally. By the first hours of Thursday morning the wind died suddenly and the vessel communities around the Lakes began the anxious wait for the weather mauled boats. 1898 was in the era of massive shipping on the Lakes, yet was also the age of telegraph communication at its best. In a three-day gale of hurricane magnitude, the fragile telegraph lines were the first victims. The best source of information then became eyewitness accounts and rumors.

At Cleveland the yacht Cygnet had been beaten to pieces, and at Alpena the Republic floated free of North Point eventually limping into port. For some reason however, Lake Michigan seemed to be the hardest hit. At Chicago, the schooner Delta was tugged in with her spars blown down. Along the city's lake front more than 81,000 dollars in damage had been done by the wind and waves. Wrecked outside of Chicago Harbor, the schooner Aloha had settled to the lake bottom. Off Racine, Wisconsin, the abandoned schooner D.L. Filer was recovered and towed into port. Those anxiously waiting for word of the missing schooner barge Pewabic were reassured to hear that she had been brought into Sheboygan with her spars, sails, anchors and deck equipment gone, but her crew in good condition. Also safe were the crewmembers of the steamer Tuttle which had gone completely to pieces at Michigan City.

In the first hours of Thursday, October 27, 1898, the steamer Louisville found the weather safe enough to push her way out of Chicago bound for St. Joseph, Michigan. At 7:00 Captain Boswell of the Louisville sighted a battered schooner rolling sluggishly in the cold gray dawn. From several miles distance he could identify the stricken schooner barge as the Olive Jeanette. Passing closer to the schooner the Louisville's crew could see that the Jeanette's masts had been blown down, and her rudder had been carried away. Although damaged, she did not appear to be in danger. So assured of the schooner's condition was the Louisville's captain that he steamed right past her and continued to St.

Joseph. Upon arrival there Captain Boswell wired Chicago reporting the approximate position of the drifting schooner, and two tugs were promptly dispatched to recover the Olive Jeanette.

After making her lines fast to a south Chicago dock the Jeanette's master, Captain D.B. Cadotte, told those ashore the story of his boat's brush with disaster. The schooner barge had departed south Chicago early Monday afternoon in tow of the wooden steamer L.R. Doty. Both boats were upbound with cargoes of grain consigned to Midland, Ontario far into Lake Huron's Georgian Bay. For nearly 24 hours the two boats battled their way into the intensifying gale. Then at five o'clock Tuesday evening, off Milwaukee, the tow line parted and the Jeanette fell off into the trough of the wild seas. Captain Cadotte watched as the Doty continued northward, head to the seas. Into the blowing sleet the big steamer slowly faded. Captain Cadotte hoped that she would make a wide circle, returning to pick his boat up, but he knew too well that there would be little chance of turning the big steamer in this kind of sea.

Figuring that he was on his own, Captain Cadotte ordered the Olive Jeanette's sails rigged. It was his good fortune that the boat was stocked with brand new canvas, and as soon as it was raised he ran for Racine, Wisconsin. For the better part of five hours the barge showed the storm her heels with the giant cresting seas slamming at her stern. Then shortly after eleven o'clock an angry wave broke her steering gear. The wind in her sails pulled the boat around into the trough of the heaving seas once again. As the barge's desperate crew scurried to make repairs to the steering gear, thundering seas repeatedly crashed aboard her decks. Soon everything on her decks, including her steam pumps and deckhouse, had been swept away. Somehow the sailors managed to re-rig the rudder tackles and the wooden schooner barge again ran before the seas. By this time however, the boat had been blown south of Racine, and being unable to turn northward into the wind, Captain Cadotte had no choice other than running south for Chicago nearly 70 miles down the churning lake.

Hours later, the Olive Jeanette had worked only a fraction of the distance to Chicago when an enraged Lake Michigan again lashed out at the barge. This time the schooner's giant oak rudder was bitten from her stern, and with it her ability to steer was completely destroyed. Through skillful manipulation of the boat's sails alone, Captain Cadotte was able to keep out of the sea trough and remain before the wind. Shortly before dawn, what should have been the death stroke came. A violent series of wind gusts burst over the boat blasting her sails to shreds. From that moment on the Jeanette was left to wallow in the trough of the killer sea. At daybreak Thursday, the storm lifted and the schooner was still afloat. Her hatches had saved her. For some unexplainable reason the hatch canvas had remained tightly sealed through the whole ordeal and barely a drop of water had found its way into her cargo.

As Captain Cadotte told his story he stopped for a moment to inquire as to the L.R. Doty's port of shelter. Surely the giant, five year old, wooden steamer had found a cozy port along the north shore and would by now be pushing her way south to recover the Olive Jeanette. After all her captain, Christopher Smith, was not one to leave loose ends unattended to. Not a man along the dock had heard of the Doty's location. The real concern had been for the Olive Jeanette, and a news release was promptly telegraphed off to the West Bay City Tribune. It read:"...The schooner Olive Jeanette was picked up off Kenosha, Wis., and brought into Chicago with all canvas and the rudder gone after weathering the gale Tuesday night. The schooner was separated from its consort, the steamer Doty, somewhere in Lake Michigan. The Doty is still out in the lake. Both boats are partially fitted with crews from this city." As the type-setter's fingers busily laid the letters of the story in the cluttered Tribune office, a much larger story was being written on the heaving surface of Lake Michigan as the steam tug Prodigy suddenly found herself pushing through a giant field of churning wreckage.

By late Thursday afternoon the Prodigy was tied up at the Chicago Independent Tug Line's dock. Captain Ebison of the steamer George Williams of the Hawgood Line, which also owned the Doty, was performing the grim task of identifying the wreckage that the Prodigy had brought in off the lake. The L.R. Doty was actually being run by the Cuyahoga Transit Company, but at this point there was no use in debating who's colors she had been flying from her fore-mast, all that remained were bits of flotsam. It was in search of the Olive Jeanette that the Prodigy had been dispatched, but when the tug was 25 miles off Kenosha, Wisconsin, she came upon a large field wreckage. At first the tug's crew thought they had found the Olive Jeanette's death smudge, but it soon became apparent that these were the remains of a giant wooden steamer. Cabin doors veneered with mahogany were the final clue. These along with a large chunk of oak deck told those on the Prodigy that one of the big, new, wooden steamers had met her fate. The tug brought the doors, some stanchions, and a pole that was painted the brown color of the Doty's hull, into the Chicago office where Captain Ebison, who had sailed the Doty, quickly identified them as being from the L.R. Doty. Finally to further seal the case of the L.R. Doty, she was the only boat on Lake Michigan that was unaccounted for.

In 1892, the Davidson shipyard at West Bay City began work on the 201 foot hull of the L.R. Doty. Over 50 acres of white oak trees were consumed in the construction of the giant steamer. When she splashed off the builder's ways into the Saginaw River the Doty carried an insurance rating of A-l, with a star, and her owners insisted that she be equipped with the best lifeboat that money could buy. Five years later she carried both to the bottom of Lake Michigan in the blink of an eye.

Perhaps it was her kind that was doomed from the start. You see, the L.R. Doty was one of six sisters, most of whom came to grief on the Lakes. Duplicates of the Doty were the Uganda, and William F. Sauber, both of whom are told of later in this text. Also sisters to the Doty were the Tampa, which was rammed and sunk on the Detroit River in 1911, then later returned to service, and the ghost ship Iosco, which vanished on Lake Superior September 3, 1905. Coincidentally, the Iosco took the Olive Jeanette to eternity with her on that stormy day. The schooner had survived the fate of one of the doomed sisters, only to "sail away" with another. Of the five sisters form the Davidson Yard only one, the C.F. Bielman, survived to work out a productive career.

The Friday evening, October 28, 1898, issue

of the Bay City Times-Press carried the grim news. "The L.R. Doty. Feared she has gone to the bottom." The same article listed the names of those thought to be gone with the Bay City boat. Captain Christopher Smith, Chief Thomas Abernethie, Mate Henry Sharpe, Second Mate W.J. Hossie, Second Engineer C.W. Odette, Oiler George Wadkin, Watchman Charles Bornie, Wheelsmen Peter G. Peterson and Albert Nelson, Firemen Joseph Fitzsimon and John Howe, Deckhands F. Harmuth, C. Curtis, William Ebart, and Pat Ryan, Cook W.J. Scott, and finally Steward Lawrence E. Goss who resided at 203 Prairie Av. in West Bay City.

Over 90 years later the events of that stormy week have been mostly forgotten, and the eyewitnesses to the gale are long dead. Of all the lakeboats that weathered the storm, only the E.M. Ford, which was formerly the Presque Isle, as of this writing, still pushes across the Lakes. The Doty's wreck, as of yet, has not been found. No monument or marker is in place to indicate her passing, all that remains of that storm and the L.R. Doty is a number on a shipwreck chart and this story.

In her career on the lakes the big wooden oreboat **L. R. Doty** was considered to be one of the finest examples of the ship builders craft. Then came the day she battled with Lake Michigan's fury. She is seen here locking upbound with what is believed to be her consort **Olive Jeanette.** Courtesy of The Great Lakes Historical Society

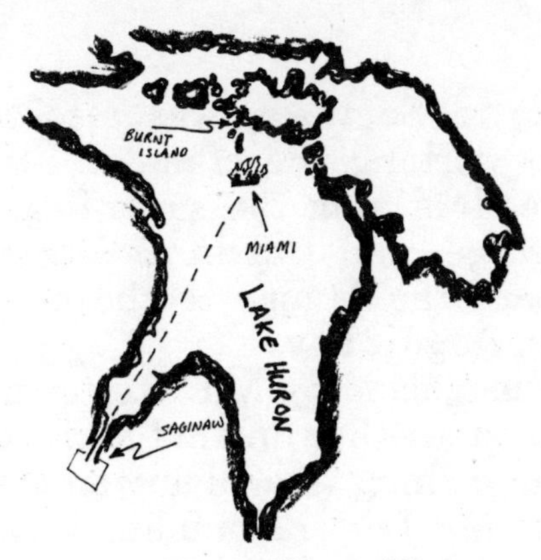

Familiar Fate

At one a.m. on the humid stuffy night of July 14, 1867 the community of Eden, New York was awakened to the cries of newly born George Godlove Heilbronn. Two hours later, George's twin, Charles Godspeed Heilbronn was delivered. Years later, the two brothers could be found gainfully employed as sailors onboard the Saginaw river's lumber fleet. Then on September 23, 1902 the sailing Heilbronn family was added to when George Heilbronn was blessed with a son, Calvin, who followed in the sailor's footsteps of his father and uncle.

At nine o'clock on the morning of August 5, 1924, the tiny wooden lumber hooker Miami chugged her way through the last of the Saginaw river's bridges. Rounding the bend, the steamer pushed out into the open bay. Onboard the Miami that warm summer morning was a crew of 12, all of whom were residents of Saginaw and Bay City. The Miami's captain, Charles Garey, who resided at 814

Kirk Street, in Saginaw, was also the vessel's owner. Also working the cramped little steamer were three sailors from the same Saginaw family. Charles, George, and Calvin Heilbronn were all serving aboard the Miami as she pushed quietly into the calm August day.

When constructed by M.P. Lester in 1888, the Miami was just another link in the working chain of lumber boats making their living on the Lakes. As she slid from Mr. Lester's building ways at Marine City the vessel was the property of the Toledo and Saginaw Transportation Company. Through the boat's long career her business seemed always to be related to the Saginaw river area, so it was only natural that her captain-owner and crew would be from this same area. With a length of 136 feet, a beam of 28 feet and a modest depth of only 9.5 feet, the Miami was perfectly suited to the twisting, shallow Saginaw river. During her first years of service, lumber boats of the Miami's size and power were a common sight around the Lakes. Now in her 36th year of service she was one of the last of her breed.

Clearing from the Saginaw river's channel, as she had done so many times before, the Miami turned northward. Lake Huron was as smooth as glass, and dozens of small pleasure boats dotted Saginaw Bay. The visibility was very poor, with a late night fog burning off into a dense summer haze by mid-morning. Running empty, the Miami was upbound to the north shore of Lake Huron. The tiny lumbering community of Sprague, Ontario, was the Miami's port of call on this trip. A twenty foot stack of rough-cut lumber was waiting to be taken back to Saginaw's mills. There it would be recut to product quality and shipped around the nation. At her snail's pace of nine miles per hour the upbound trip would take the aging Miami nearly thirty hours to complete.

Throughout the hot August day and a shimmering night, the creaking, musty, old wooden boat hissed her way north into Lake Huron. Life onboard the Miami was a good deal different from that of the average giant steel lakeboat running in 1924. There was no sparkling galley, instead there was a small dining table adjacent to a wood burning cookstove. A few large cast iron pots were used to cook and clean up after every meal. The crew quarters were cramped and there was no such thing as a shower. Why then would the three sailing members of the Heilbronn family choose to work the grimy back waters of the Great Lakes onboard the Miami, instead of the fresh blue long haul runs onboard one of those modern steel giants? Perhaps it was the same reason that drew Eli Putnam, Joseph Collett, and Walter Chambers, all of whom were from Bay City, to the Miami. Exactly the same reason that drew Elmer Pittman, Perry Fray, Kenneth Davis, Albert Kast, and Orville Miller, all of Saginaw, to Captain Garey's boat. Those blue water longhauls terminated at distant ports such as Cleveland, Lorain, Marquette, and Duluth. All of these ports were far from home and signing aboard one of the longhaul boats, in these days before sailor's unions and mandatory vacations could mean spending more than eight months away from home and family. While the dilapidated Miami steamed far into the filthy Saginaw river on a regular basis, and whether she tied up in east Saginaw or west Bay City, the off duty crew members were able to beat a quick path to their own front doors.

Another difference between a wooden boat and the big steel boats was that one particular word struck fear into the heart of a wooden vesselman much more than it could any sailor of steelboats. The word was "fire" and since the advent of the wooden steamboat, countless vessels had been consumed to the waterline by swift flame and choking smoke. Since the Frontenac was destroyed on the Niagara river in 1827, more than 80 steamers had burned to a smoldering hulk on the Great Lakes by the time the 1924 season opened. Normally the seeds of flaming destruction would sprout aft. Sparks belched from the steamer's tall stack would find their way into some obscure nook in the boat's wooden superstructure. Smoldering for hours, the sparks would soon turn to flames, and within minutes the entire vessel would be hopelessly involved. Many times the survivors of a burning steamer would testify that the flames had begun on the deckhouse roof, and most commonly, between the stack and the superstructure. In the era of the wooden steamboat, demise by fire was an all too familiar fate.

It was shortly before one o'clock in the afternoon on August 6, 1924, when Coal Passer Albert Kast finished his lunch in the Miami's cramped galley. Calvin Heilbronn and Orville Miller, also members of the engineroom crew, remained behind picking at the last of their lunches. Stepping from the galley, Kast planted both hands on the boat's stern rail. The day was warm with a dense haze hanging over the glassy lake. It was then that he noticed a pungent odor unlike any other he had smelled before. The smell was that of smoke, but not the normal smoke produced by the steamer's boilers, or the galley's cookstove. Curious, Kast followed his nose to the source of the smell. His curiosity led him to the large hold where the boat's coal fuel was stored. A wisp of smoke was creeping from between the big clumps of black coal. To Kast's astonishment the wisp of smoke quickly turned into a thick black billow before his eyes. The Miami's coal bunkers, which extended from her spar deck, down nearly to her bottom, were on fire. A heart-beat later, Kast burst into the galley doorway shouting that one word that told every crewmember within earshot that their boat was doomed... "FIRE."

The series of shouts, and a thundering of feet running across the Miami's wooden deck soon drew every member of the boat's crew out to fight the rapidly growing fire. Buckets attached to ropes were repeatedly tossed into the lake, then drawn up to her deck so that water could be tossed onto the smoking coal bunker. In the pilothouse Captain Garey rang "stop" on the boat's chadburn. Stopping the boat would aid in preventing the fire from spreading. At the boat's stern accommodations, the smoke was getting quite thick. Half a dozen crewmen were mustered on a steam hose which would normally be used to steam away hull ice picked up in winter storms. Now, the steam would be used to fight the combustion in the coal bunker. Below decks another hose was being rigged to the boat's pumps. By the time the hose was rigged and on deck, flames were leaping from the bunker and the boat's aft accommodations were beginning to combust. Realizing that the Miami's wooden life boats were atop the deckhouse, and that those accommodations would be shortly consumed, Captain Garey ordered the boats launched and pulled to the bow.

Steam from the boilers, water from the pumps, and sweat from the crew did no good toward saving the steamer. The choking smoke swallowed the entire stern of the Miami. The flames curled from the after cabin, and began to work their way forward along the boat's empty cargo hold. Those crewmen housed forward ran to their cabins to grab as many of their personal possessions as their hands could quickly pack. For the three Heilbronns, and all those who made their home away from home in the Miami's after quarters, it was already too late to save their personal effects. Everything, with the exception of the clothing they were wearing, was going up in smoke.

From the time the first wisp of smoke was discovered by Albert Kast until the last member of the steamer's crew stepped into the lifeboat, only 90 minutes had passed. Tall orange flames burst from her hull, as the yawl pulled away from the burning Miami, the sailors could feel the heat radiating across the open lake. All that the crew could do now was row for dry land. The problem was that in their haste in abandoning the burning Miami, none of her crew had bothered to look at the boat's compass to see which direction land was. The lifeboat was lacking a compass, and the thick haze shrouded any sight of land in the distance. Captain Garey estimated their position as being about 11 miles south of Straits, and judging by the late afternoon sun, the sailors pulled in the direction he assumed to be north. Soon the Miami was nothing more than a spear of brownish gray smoke rising through the distant haze.

Across the open face of northern Lake Huron the boatless sailors rowed their tiny yawl. There was little doubt that they were headed in approximately the right direction, soon they should hit Great Duck Island. At worst, in a week or so they would hit Port Huron. An hour passed, and then two hours as the Miami's crew quietly rowed along. At half past five o'clock in the evening the fishing tug Edna A. came upon the shipwrecked sailors.

Pulling alongside the Yawl, the Edna A.'s crew were quite astonished to find a lifeboat full of sailors amid such calm weather. A single whiff of their smoke saturated clothing told an all too familiar story. Puffing along with her catch of the day, the fishing tug headed for the tiny village of Burnt Island that was her destination.

The following morning, the Edna A. took the shipwrecked sailors to Cheboygan, Michigan. There all of the crew with the exception of the boat's captain and engineer, caught the Detroit and Northern train for Bay City. The trip down brought a coach load of grimy sailors with only the clothes on their backs left in their possession. When the three Heilbronns got back to their Saginaw homes, the time that it would have taken the Miami to make a normal trip to Sprague had elapsed, but the news of the boat's burning had not yet reached the Saginaw area. When the Heilbronn men returned home they were nonchalantly greeted as if they had just completed another day's work. Those three sailors then had the awkward task of informing their kinfolk that because of the Miami, the whole family was temporarily unemployed.

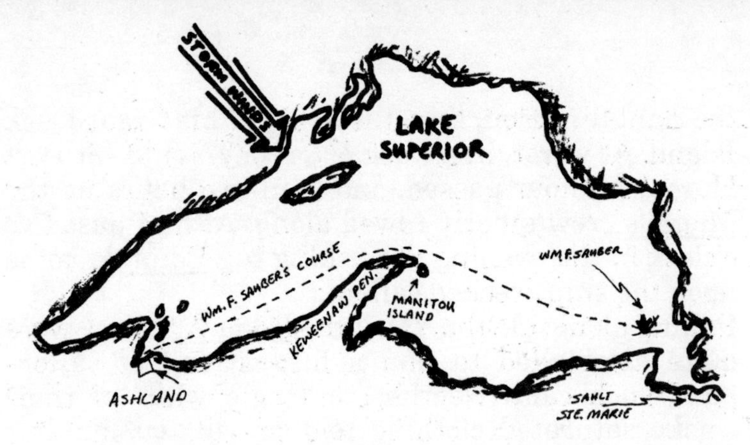

The Wooden Boat And The Iron Man

A large crowd had gathered at the F.W. Wheeler boatyard on a brisk April 15, 1891. From all over west Bay City the people had grouped for another boat launching. When the giant 300 foot wooden hull slid down the ways the crowd would stand and cheer. Hull number 78 represented another profitable job completed by the Saginaw river's thriving ship-building industry. It was a single beat in the heart of the Bay City economy. Officially measuring 291 feet in keel (310 overall), 41 feet in beam and 19.8 feet in depth, Hull 78 was 2,053 gross tons burden. Cleveland's Mitchell & Company, owners of Hull 78, had contracted for a triple expansion steam engine to be put into their new boat. Constructed at Frontier Iron Works in Detroit, the giant steam engine would have a 20, 32, and 54 inch diameter by 42 inch stroke. Painted proudly on the bow and stern of Hull 78 as it splashed into the murky brown water of the Saginaw river was the name William F. Sauber.

It is often said that the era of the William F. Sauber was one of wooden ships and iron men, in fact the turn of the century was a time of great contrast on the lakes. Wooden freighters and lumber hookers numbering in the hundreds were sailing around the lakes. Sailing schooners and schooner barges could be found everywhere. Whalebacks were mixed with wooden car ferries on the lower lakes, and spanking new steel freighters were gaining a foothold. A daily passage at Port Huron could number more than 60 vessels. The boat watcher would see vessels that nearly a century later would be famous, or infamous. A good example would be the last day of July, 1903, a parade of lakeboats including the William F. Sauber were transiting the crowded waterway connecting Lake Huron and Lake Erie. Reported downbound were names such as John J. McWilliams (one of the early steel steamers constructed at Bay City's F. W. Wheeler shipyard), Castle Rhodes, M.A. Hanna, Saginaw, Sir Henry Bessemer, and Thomas Bangor. Also snoring down the river came the Ed Smith towing her consort, followed closely by the composite steamer Manchester that would later gain fame under the name Yankcannuck as the last composite boat on the lakes. The steamers Manola, Frank W. Hart, D.G. Kerr, William E. Reis, Maryland, and H.E. Runnels followed. In tow of a small puffing tug the schooner Penobscot passed downbound followed by the steamer Mars and Rensselser.

Looking like a surfaced submarine, the whaleback steamer Frank Rockefeller towing the barge Maida, both under the colors of the Steel

Trust of the Pittsburgh steamship Company, chugged downbound. The Rockefeller would end her days as the museum ship Meteor moored at Barkers Island 70 years later, with tourists walking her decks. After the steamers Wilbur and Sesquehanna, another team of the Steel Trust's whalebacks snored down toward the lower lakes. They were the Henry Cort and her whaleback consort. Finishing up the day's passage down were the Manhattan, Pueblo, Venus, the steel hulled D.M. Whitney and the steamers Antrim, F.M. Osborne, Centurion, and Codorus.

Pushing upbound toward the open lake on that sticky July day were another 57 boats. Far south near Detroit the Walter Scranton was following the steel lumber hooker Charles S. Neff who in turn was following that Andaste which 26 years later would vanish with all hands on Lake Michigan. Working north were the Lambert following the W.D. Rees which was plowing behind the Zenith City. The Miami and her consort pushed their way up behind the Harvard, Sinaola, John Ericsson, Orinoco, India, Colonel, James H. Hoyt, and Scranton. This was the fleet upbound from Detroit to the lower St. Clair river.

From the upper St. Clair river south to Lake St. Clair the remainder of the fleet consisted of the Oglebay followed by the Frank Peavey, Buffalo, Arizona and barges Pratt, and Athens. The Maggie Duncan steamed ahead of the Fred Mercur, and Grecian. Pushing up behind the Grecian came an illfated pair, the steamer Iosco with the barge Olive Jeanette. Both would vanish with all hands on Lake Superior two years later. Following them came the Brittanie, Averell, Simon J. Murphy, Lake Shores, Siberia, Maruba, and right in the middle of the whole days traffic was the wooden _William F. Sauber_ with her iron master, William E. Morris, standing in her pilothouse.

When looking at a photo of Captain Morris, one sees the stern face of a man who took great pride in his duty as a master of vessels. A man who found his charge as captain of the _William F. Sauber_ to be more of a natural way of life than a burden of responsibility. It is doubtless that the good captain would stand firmly on the white oak decks of the _Sauber_ and scoff at the giant steel steamers as they slid past in the summer sun. Late that evening on the last day of July, 1903, on the open lake the _Sauber_ passed near another of that new breed of steel steamers and the iron men of the wooden boat scoffed again, much as sailors today scoff at the new 730 foot self-unloaders. "That's not real steamboating," they murmured to one another as the 428 foot _Presque Isle_ hissed past them downbound, "Damn things'll never last on the lakes." Over 93 years later the _Presque Isle_ could be seen sailing proudly as Huron Cement's _E.M. Ford_, the oldest bulk steamer on earth. Even knowing the _Presque Isle's_ future could not have changed the opinions of Captain Morris and the other iron men onboard the _William F. Sauber_. They really had no use for the giant steel boats that could haul four times as much cargo as the _Sauber_, and might put them all out of a job, no use at all.

A little less than three months later, fall was turning quickly to winter on the Lakes. It had been a stormy October, and as early as the middle of the month the ore was freezing in the loading pockets at Ashland. A late October gale had been blowing for nearly five days and the _Sauber's_ loading had been hindered by the frozen ore refusing to tumble down the shoots into her hold. Saturday morning October 24, 1903, revealed another deep gray wind-racked day. Sporadic bursts of hard snow dusted the harbor. Giant waves of icewater slapped onto the shore; Lake Superior was out of sorts today.

Just after one o'clock in the afternoon, the last of the frozen ore clunked into the white oak hull of the Sauber. It took the better part of an hour for her crew to secure her hatches. Captain Morris proudly guided his charge from under the loading pier, pushing into a firm northwest wind the Sauber cleared Ashland at three o'clock in the afternoon. Rolling gently in the big swells the boat was taking some water on her decks, but was making good weather. There was no reason to delay sailing today, after all the weather that Captain Morris had guided his boat through on the upbound trip had been much more nasty. An hour later the watch had changed and the Sauber's iron master retired quietly to his quarters. In the Sauber's era, it was unheard of to give sailors mandatory days of vacations for a given number of days worked . From the opening of the season in March until season's close in December the boat was not only a place of work but it was their home. On this windy evening of October, home was pushing through the open lake at her normal pace of just over 10 miles per hour.

Rounding the Keweenaw Point the Sauber and her crew came abeam Manitou Island. It was nine a.m., just 18 hours after she'd cleared Ashland. That firm northwest wind suddenly blasted over the steamer bringing snow and ice pellets with it. Those rolling waves soon turned into giant gray combers. In his quarters Captain Morris was jolted from his breakfast as his boat smashed her bluff bow into the growing seas. When he reached the pilothouse

Captain Morris found the wind blowing a full gale off his boat's stern quarter. The Sauber was already cork-screwing heavily in the seas, her oak timbers groaning loudly with each wave.

Perhaps it was the good captain's confidence in the boat that influenced his next decision, or perhaps it was his iron stubbornness to complete another trip in spite of Lake Superior. When discretion would have told most masters of wooden boats to simply round the Keweenaw and shelter behind the point, Captain Morris directed the Sauber to continue on her course for Whitefish Bay. Rather than waste time squatting in the protected waters to the south, the iron master had winked at nature's fury and would soon pay the price.

Shortly before four o'clock p.m. First Mate Alexander McRae went below to check the boat's hold. Not to his surprise he found a respectable amount of water splashing about. This fact he reported promptly to Captain Morris who ordered the pumps started. About an hour later McRae returned to the hold to find more water and several seams leaking. The boat's cork-screwing action in the big waves had sprung her planking and Lake Superior was gaining on the pumps. Now McRae ran to the pilothouse and reported the leaking to Captain Morris. This was the moment to turn and run for shelter behind the Keweenaw, but the iron captain pushed his wooden boat on toward White Fish Point. Less than a half hour later the first mate found the water in the hold to be nearly up to his chest. In the firehold water was sloshing freely at the ankles of the engineroom crew. McRae's conclusion was one that no one could deny, the William F. Sauber was sinking.

By the time nightfall gripped a churning Lake

Superior, the Sauber was hoisting distress signals and her steam whistle hooted a series of distress pleas into the wild blackness of the storm. Her crew gave their big oak freighter less than a few hours survival time in the tremendous seas. Soon the icy water would overtake her pumps and finish the Sauber. In this maelstrom the crew could take to the lifeboats and still be swallowed by Lake Superior. The Sauber would then become just another vessel that vanished without witness.

In the way of things on the Lakes, sometimes what you have the most contempt for turns out to be what you may one day have the most use for. In the case of the iron master of the foundering Sauber, what he needed most tonight turned out to be one of big steel steamers that he so often scoffed at. From out of the darkness rolled the lights of the steel freighter Yale. The Sauber was no longer alone on the open Lake.

From the Yale's pilothouse Captain James Jackson scanned the wooden steamer's hull with his spotlight and could readily see that the Sauber's condition was dire. Being beaten by the wind and seas, it appeared that if the ravaged wooden boat did not find shelter she would surely plunge to Lake Superior's bottom. The nearest shelter however, was White Fish Point nearly 70 miles ahead. At her current wallowing rate of six miles per hour she would never make it. In fact it appeared that the freighter would sink before the Yale could reach her. The master of the Yale reasoned that if the Sauber could not get to shelter, he would do the next best thing and bring shelter to her. Pulling the big steel hull of the Yale up along side the leaking Sauber he would use his boat as a wind break. Perhaps Captain Jackson could buy enough time for the

Sauber to limp around Whitefish Point. On the other hand, if he maneuvered the Yale too close to the tender wooden steamer the two boats may strike one another sending the heavily laden Sauber to her doom in a matter of seconds. It was a risky proposition, but this was a desperate time. As the Yale pulled upwind of the Sauber, the crest of the thrashing seas calmed slightly, now the boat had a fighting chance against the lake. Below, in the engine room the intruding lake water would slosh against the hot boiler workings. Steam filled the air, breathing was difficult, and Chief Engineer Everett Butler ordered Firemen Bernard Brown and Jim Gallagher to shovel for their lives. Mate McRae had told the chief to keep the steam up, but to also be ready to take to the boats at any moment. It was nothing that Butler hadn't figured out on his own. The ash blackened water that soaked him nearly to the hips and filled the firehold with choking clouds of steam were enough to tell him that the Sauber was doomed.

Hours of darkness passed and the wooden boat from West Bay City wallowed lower and lower into the cold lake. Beside her the Yale paced, waiting for the Sauber to founder, or survive. Captain Jackson and every available hand on the Yale fixed their attention on the leaking boat, watching for the first sign of her crew abandoning. In the William F. Sauber's pilothouse Captain Morris stood rock solid, as if his will and authority alone could get his boat, his responsibility, and his home into Whitefish Bay.

Shortly before three o'clock a.m. on Monday, October 26, 1903 the Sauber rolled steeply dipping her beam end into the sea. Green water shipped aboard and Captain Morris knew at once that the end was at hand. Turning to First Mate McRae, who was trying to regain his balance on the windowsill, he gave his last stoic order. "Bring up the engine room crew and man the yawls...Leave the boat." Then he reached down and grabbed the boat's brass whistle-pull, giving the abandon ship signal. Taking the Sauber's big wooden wheel in his own hands, Captain Morris then ordered Wheelsman Carl Johnson to take to the boats as well.

Dashing across the swamped deck was no easy task. The sinking steamer was down nearly to her scuppers and each wave washed over the rolling boat waist deep to her struggling crew as the freighter continued to steam full ahead toward her doom. Aft atop the deckhouse, scurrying sailors were attempting to launch the port lifeboat. Ordinarily in this kind of weather, the launching of the boats would have been nearly impossible. Numb hands fumble with the lashings, cresting waves sweep away bodies, and the tearing frozen wind bites like a giant monster, hampering the frantic efforts of a doomed crew. Tonight however, the wall-like hull of the Yale blocked the wind and subdued the waves. Over the side went the yawl. All of the Sauber's crew crowded in, with the exclusion of Captain Morris who was still holding his boat the proper distance from the Yale. Once the lifeboat was filled with the Sauber's shivering crew First Mate McRae left his seat and fought his way to the pilothouse to get the captain. A few frozen minutes later, McRae struggled back to the waiting yawl. Without a word, he indicated to continue lowering away, Captain Morris was not coming.

Pitching in the heavy seas the lifeboat nearly swamped several times on the way over to the waiting Yale. When the Sauber's crew reached the safety of the big steel steamer, a rope was tossed down to the shipwrecked sailors. One by one, they were hoisted to the Yale's deck. All were saved with the exception of Oiler Frank Robinson, who slipped from safety and was swallowed by Lake Superior.

From the fence of the Yale, William Crocker, Everett Butler, Theodore Vanderhike, Ole Dryus, Carl Johnson, Julius Werts, Bert Fraser, Bernard Brown, James Gallagher, and Alexander McRae watched silently as the William F. Sauber went down by the head. Lifting her stern high into the air, her big screw could be seen still turning. As Lake Superior's icewater contacted the boat's red hot boiler's there was a thunderous explosion that wiped clean the boat's stern. The boat plunged below the churning lake, just 30 miles short of Whitefish Point's shelter.

The following afternoon the Yale pulled into the Soo locks and dropped off the Sauber's people. First Mate McRae immediately telegraphed William Becker in Cleveland. His message was brief, the 80,000 dollar wooden freighter and her iron master were gone. The question of why Captain Morris went down with his boat was not addressed that day, he was just gone and that was all.

Some writers like to romanticize about sailing "tradition" and captains always going down with the ship. This rubbish certainly is not applicable to the Lakes. Normally, captains leave their boats with their crews when foundering is inevitable. There is the rare instance or two where an unstable personality causes a despondent master to go down with the ship, but this was not Captain Morris' situation. Why then did Captain Morris go to his doom on the Sauber? While some history books write romantically of the traditional captain going down with his ship, and others speak of a confused frantic man unable to give up his charge, This history book will not speculate on those far reaching lines. The simple fact is that Captain William E. Morris held the William F. Sauber safely off the Yale as his crew got clear and to safety. In the boat's worst moment she had to be guided by the most capable hands onboard, those of her captain. No romance, no despondence, no panic, simply the common sense of an iron man.

Triskaidekaphobia

There were only 12 and one half shopping days remaining before Christmas Day, 1963 as WLB-406, the United States Coast Guard Cutter Acacia, steamed silently into Saginaw Bay. On the fantail of the 180 foot cutter a seaman carefully fastened the boat's American flag to the vessel's flag pole. Flapping in the cold wind, the stars and stripes were hoisted all the way to the top of the pole then lowered to half mast in honor of President John F. Kennedy who had recently fallen to an assassin's bullet.

The Acacia's chore for the next few days would be the removal of the lighted buoys marking the Saginaw Bay and River. This would be a cold, wet, numbing task required to spare the buoys from the crushing shifting ice of winter. The 1963 shipping season was rapidly drawing to a close on the Saginaw River and Mother Nature seemed to be impatiently crowding the Great Lakes for the season's termination. Even as the 1025 ton Acacia was preparing to lift buoys, a powerful low pressure system was sweeping down out of the Canadian Arctic. Centered now over the Soo, the front arced all the way down into mid-Texas. A hard snow was falling as far down as Tennessee, Georgia and South Carolina. Over 85 percent of the continental United States was below the freezing mark. Ice and snow quickly began to choke the Great Lakes.

Winter lay-up was in full swing among the vast fleet of lakeboats. At Rogers City, for example, the Bradly Transportation Line's gray hulls were going to winter quarters. Captain J.H. Parrilla announced to the media that their season would end before Christmas. The entire fleet would go to the wall between December 21 and 23. Wintering at Rogers City would be the steamers John G. Munson, Cedarville, Rogers City, T.W. Robinson and Myron C. Taylor. Going to Lorain, Ohio for re-powering to a diesel engine would be the steamer Calcite II. The steamer Irvin L. Clymer would also be spending the winter in the American Ship Building Company's yard at Lorain being spruced-up.

"One more trip" is the late season problem that lakeboats often face in the closing days of every shipping season. In the final hour of Thursday, the 12th of December 1963, Columbia Steamship Line's 428 foot crane boat Buckeye was bound into Saginaw Bay with a load for the Saginaw Grey Iron Foundry. This late season passage would just about end a long season of very hard work for this tired old steamer. Hauling assorted bulk cargoes up the foul, brackish, industrial backwaters of the Great Lakes is a far cry from the job the boat was intended for when she slid off the ways at the Detroit

Shipbuilding Company in 1901. Her hull then had the name D.M. Whitney painted on it and her task was carrying longhaul ore and coal. Her career on the fresh blue water of the open lakes was without major incident. The steamer's single claim to fame happened on June 15, 1931, when as the Thomas Britt she became the first vessel to pass down the Welland canal after it was opened to vessels of 450 feet in length. By 1963 two giant cranes had been added to the old boat's spar deck. The name Buckeye was now on her bow and stern and she was spending her golden years servicing the foundries and industrial docks that were tucked deep inland and not accessible to larger vessels. After 62 uneventful seasons of operation, triskaidekaphobia, or the superstitious fear of the number 13, was unknown to the Buckeye as she lined up on a heading for the mouth of the Saginaw River. Three hours later, she passed the cutter Acacia, it was just before 2 a.m. on Friday the 13th.

Passage anywhere on the lakes had been particularly difficult in the fall of 1963 due to the water-level on all five lakes being at its lowest point since 1933. Lake Huron was at 575.82 feet above sea level. The lake level had dropped two inches in thirty days. Normally the drop during this time of year is less than one tenth of one inch. A boat being troubled by this low water would be unlucky to say the least, but this circumstance alone would be no reason to come down with a case of triskaidekaphobia. At about the same time that the aging Buckeye started inbound, a 30 mile per hour southwest wind began to scream over Saginaw Bay. Wind in this direction pushes the water in the bay out into the open lake and thus pulls the water level in the river down to exceptionally low levels.

The bones of more that 26 abandoned wooded vessels along the river make a ghostly appearance.

Blizzard warnings were out for Bay City and Saginaw as the Buckeye gingerly entered the shallow river. Along the shoreline the flashing amber lights of an army of snow plows could hardly be seen through the thick snowfall. On the river the darkness was pierced by the white stiletto beam of the Buckeye's probing searchlight. Checked down to a snails crawl, the steamer made her way though the snow-chocked darkness. It was a balmy 15 degrees outside. Shortly before six a.m. the boat slipped though the sulking black-iron D and N railroad bridge. Turning on the right wheel the boat lined up in mid-channel a few points to starboard. With the first bridge in the long winding river behind her the Buckeye now pointed toward the old Belinda Street Bridge.

The change in the boat's motion was nearly undetectable as the steamer slowly came to a silent halt. After a short pause the boat's screw began to churn the mud and ice as the vessel's master attempted to back her. The big boat refused to budge. A mudbank in mid channel had a firm grip on the 62 year old steamer and was not about to let her go. This Friday the 13th was not only casting a handful of bad luck toward the Buckeye, but was also sprinkling a touch of triskaidekaphobia on Boland and Cornelius's 532 foot self-unloader Ben W. Calvin. The big steamer was not only caught in the storm, but had also become stuck in the ice on Saginaw Bay. This trip to the Wirt Stone Dock was to be her last of the season. In fact, she was to lay-up in Bay City at the Defoe Ship Yard, but a last minute order from the home office in Buffalo directed her to winter in Toledo instead. Now she would have to call on the Acacia to stop her buoy lifting chore and aid the Calvin into the river. Once there her problem would be getting past the grounded Buckeye which was stuck firmly in mid-channel.

Daylight was a dark gray sky and a series of snow squalls that came and went without end. There in the river directly opposite the Bay City Municipal Sewage Plant and a scant 100 yards short of the Belinda Street bridge the Buckeye sat hissing clouds of white vent steam and belching black smoke from her stack. For hours the boat's big wheel had churned the river as her rudder swung from side to side, but the mudbank aided by the wind and low water continued to hold her fast. By mid-morning two tugs were called her aid. Lines were put aboard the crane boat and the tugs groaned and pulled on the steamer. Soon nearly every direction had been tried but the Buckeye refused to move. By the late afternoon, most of her crew had come to the conclusion that they would have either have to wait for the river level to come back up when the wind shifted or wait for Friday the 13th to come to an end before their boat could sail on.

Darkness seemed to fall early that evening and along with it the temperature plummeted toward the single digits. That stiff southwest wind continued to blow steadily across the Saginaw River and Bay at peaks of over 30 miles per hour. Over five inches of snow had now been heaped on the area. In the middle of all this winter the old Buckeye sat, frosted like a cake. Ashore that evening, the old boat's embarrassment had not gone unnoticed. The Bay City Times carried a large photo of the poor steamer with the simple caption "freighter runs aground...." After decades of steaming up and down the Saginaw River unnoticed the old boat was now the object of dinner-time news. It was the nasty weather alone that spared her from crowds of onlookers with pointing fingers.

Onboard, her crew was doing what lakeboat sailors must all be able to do, waiting. Tonight it was waiting for the wind to change, waiting for the river to come back up, waiting for the boat to float free, waiting to finish this trip and for the season to end. All aboard the steamer knew that the tugs that had been called to her aid could pull with all their might, but as with all boats that sail the Lakes, it is Mother Nature who dictates how and when this trip would end.

It was shortly before 10 p.m. and just over two hours before Friday the 13th would end when the wind suddenly died, then shifting nearly 180 degrees, blew hard out of the northeast. The brown murky river water began to rise rapidly and by 11 p.m. the Buckeye floated free. Pushing again slowly forward the old crane boat passed a snow covered downtown Bay City at midnight. Friday the 13th was over. Behind the Buckeye, the Ben W. Calvin snored through the Belinda Street Bridge. A thick white coat of ice covered the big self-unloader from bow to stern. It was easy to see that the Calvin's Friday the 13th out on the open bay had not been pleasant. Arriving at the Saginaw grey iron foundry just after four a.m. the boat's big whirly cranes began to pile her cargo shore-side. The Buckeye had tasted the mud once again on her way in. This time it was just past the Zilwaulkee Bridge, but she managed to free herself in a half hour and proceeded to the grey iron dock. Perhaps her luck had changed, or perhaps the inclinations of Mother

Nature were now more on the boat's side.

In the pitch black of Saturday night the 14th of December, 1963 the Buckeye cleared Saginaw Bay, several hours behind the Ben W. Calvin, who's lay-up port had now been changed to Toledo. This closed the season for the Saginaw River and put an end to one of the last chapters of the old Buckeye. In 1968 the old boat was put to scrap after having been idle for several years. Today all that remains of the Buckeye's brush with triskaidekaphobia is a large yellowing photo in the files of the Bay Country Historical Museum. In the picture the Buckeye sits in midriver smoking and steaming. On the back is scrawled "Buckeye I, stuck in the mud due to low water level, December, 13, 1963."

Trapped by mud and bad luck the **Buckeye** waits for Friday the 13th to end.

Courtesy of Historical Museum of Bay County

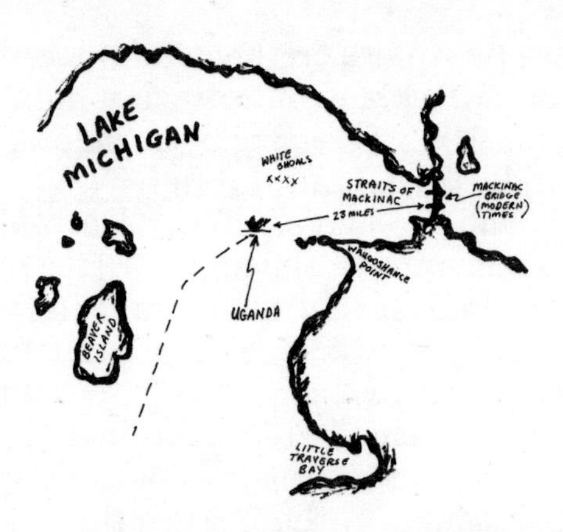

White Oaks and Sheet Ice

As the winter skies began to clear to spring in the first days of April, 1913, Edward Mehi was looking toward a productive season for his wooden steam boat Uganda. The season would begin with a few hauls of iron ore to replenish the dwindling winter stockpiles along the lower Lakes. Upbound cargoes would be of coal to feed the frostbitten villages on the upper Lake shores. Most prominently, however the Uganda would haul the cargo that had become her mainstay...grain. From the winter storage elevators all around the Lakes a wave of corn, wheat, oats, and a thousand other grades of grain needed to be shipped to the hungry eastern cities of the United States. It was while performing the task of hauling grain that the wooden freighter was at her best. Her oak hull seemed always to ride nicely with it onboard. Mr.

Mehi had kept his pencils extra busy during the frozen, gray winter in order to provide a good season's schedule of work for his boat; he had booked nearly two dozen cargoes.

The Uganda was a Bay City boat, constructed at the F.W.Wheeler yard in 1892. With a depth of 19 feet, a beam of 41 feet, and a keel length of 291 feet, she was one of the last of six nearly identical sisters. From this half dozen boats only three, including the Uganda, would be opening the 1913 season. The steamers Tampa and C.F. Bielman would be active in the grain trade along with their sister ship. Never to be seen again in any trade were the three other sisters. In 1905 the Uganda's sister boat Iosco vanished with all hands off Point Abbaye in Lake Superior along with the schooner barge Olive Jeanette. Two years earlier the William F. Sauber, another of the sisters sank 30 miles west of Whitefish Point. In 1898 the L.R. Doty was whipped from the face of Lake Michigan. She too was an identical sister to the Uganda. Coincidentally, the Doty was also towing the Olive Jeanette, but that day the ill-fated schooner barge survived. When the Uganda splashed into the brackish Saginaw River on April 12, 1892, she was among doomed sisters.

It was just past noon, nearly 21 years to the day that the Uganda was launched, when the last bushel of corn was put into her hold at Milwaukee, Wisconsin. Her crew closed the hatches neatly over the 100,000 bushels that were consigned to Buffalo, New York. On that Friday the 18th day of April, 1913, most of the ice was clear of the lower lake ports. Cold gray fog mixed with a shivering rain blustered around the Uganda as she crouched below the towering grain elevator. Captain Crockett took his place in snug warmth of the pilothouse just after two o'clock in the afternoon.

A large blanket of thick black smoke from the Uganda's tall stack choked the docks near the elevator. Slowly her big screw began to churn the water astern, and the boat began to angle from against the pier. At half past two, the wooden steamer cleared Milwaukee and pushed her way into Lake Michigan. Onboard, her crew settled in for the four day trip to Buffalo. Pushing into Lake Michigan's choppy sea the Uganda picked up her standard pace of 10 miles per hour.

Winter is always late in giving up its frozen grip on the Straits of Mackinaw. Late into the month of April, the narrow Straits remain choked with late season ice floes. This is the normal rite of spring that Great Lakes' sailors take in stride as part of the opening of each season's navigation. Giant sheets of ice miles across wander with the wind in and out of the shipping lanes having no regard for the big boats that must push through. At times the prevailing west winds will cram the ice floes into the bottleneck of the narrow straits bringing navigation to a standstill. Saturday found the Uganda still pounding northward on Lake Michigan, and it was nearly dusk when the oak steamer hauled around toward the east on a heading through the Straits of Mackinaw to Lake Huron.

Behind the Uganda came the five year old steel steamer John A. Donaldson. Opening her season with a passage through the straits, the 400 foot long Donaldson was well able to cope with any late season ice. Her steel hull was about 150 to 124 feet shorter than the standard lakeboat running in 1913, but she was still quite profitable. On this day, while steaming a couple of miles behind the Uganda, the Donaldson was about to take on the most important role of her career.

As the Uganda approached White Shoals at the westernmost end of the Mackinaw Straits, she began to encounter a great deal of ice. The floes became more and more numerous until they formed a solid white sheet across the surface of the water. Checking his boat's speed down, Captain Crockett surveyed the ice field. Apparently loosely packed, the floes weren't anything that the wooden steamer would have any problems pushing through. Moving slow ahead, the Uganda began the noisy process of crunching her way through the Straits. The oak timbers used on these wooden steamers were extremely hard, and as the Uganda broke her way east, the heavy planking in her bow was more than a match for Lake Michigan's ice.

Cramming deep into the ice pack the big wooden freighter slowly began to lose forward way until it ground to a halt. After a brief pause, the Uganda backed up along the path she had just cut. Stopping about three boat length's back, the steamer again started forward toward the waiting ice. Gaining momentum as she charged ahead the boat shoved her way deeper into the pack. Once more the wooden Uganda crunched to a stop. Apparently repeated stabs at the ice would be required if the boat were to force her way through to open water. The sheet ice had folded upon itself forming windrows and the Uganda was going to have a more difficult time than Captain Crockett had anticipated.

Pushing backward for another run at the ice-choked Straits, the Uganda shuddered to an unexpected stop. At first her Master thought nothing of the muffled jolt that had just rocked his vessel, but as the boat started forward to resume breaking ice, she began to show a slight list. By the time her bow re-engaged the ice-pack the boat's chief reported that there was water below. Less than a half hour later, all of the boat's pumps were working, but the steamer was quickly settling aft. The cargo hold was now rapidly filling with water. Her pumps had been overcome and in less than an hour the situation was hopeless. Distress signals were echoed across the lake as another of the doomed sisters began to slip below the water.

Near the stricken Uganda, the steel Donaldson was breaking her way through the same pack of ice. Alerted to the wooden steamer's plight, the Donaldson began to chip her way toward the sinking steamer. By the time Donaldson reached the Uganda the lake was nearly up to the wooden boat's spar deck.

Atop the aft quarters of the Uganda her crew was preparing to lower the lifeboat toward the ice below. It was rather an odd use for the boats, after all they were intended to be launched into water and waves in order to keep a shipwrecked crew afloat. Now the yawls would play the role of elevator, taking the Uganda's crew down to the rough sheet ice surrounding the boat. In an awkward operation of floating, pulling, walking, and dragging, all 22 members of the Uganda's crew made their way to the waiting Donaldson. By the use of the steel steamer's own lifeboats, the luckless vesselmen were hoisted to the rescue boat's deck.

Fearing that the inrush of cold water striking the wooden steamer's hot boilers would cause a violent explosion, the Donaldson quickly began to back away from the Uganda. An explosion of this kind could result in a concussion and some flying shrapnel that might damage the Donaldson. Even with this in mind, both the crews of the Donaldson and Uganda lined the rescue boat's rail to watch the white oak Bay City boat go down. Settling stern first, the Uganda slid rapidly through the ice, then began a sudden plunge. The air trapped in her bow compressed and suddenly blew the forward accommodations from the boat. Wreckage from the boat's deckhouse flew into the air and settled like confetti onto the ice. As the vessel vanished below, a giant hill of churning, bubbling water formed in her place. A sound like that of distant thunder rolled across the Donaldson.

In the quiet that followed the Uganda's spectacular death, the crew that she left behind, aboard the Donaldson stood looking at one another in an empty silence. Not only were they without a boat, but they were now unemployed. It had taken just two and one half hours, from the time the boat backed to make her last cut until she slipped below the lake at 8 p.m.. The following day, Captain Beggs brought the Donaldson into Port Huron and dropped off the Uganda's crew. Now Captain Crockett had the unpleasant task of wiring Mr. Mehi and informing him that the productive season that he had worked so hard to put together during the long winter had come to an abrupt end in the Straits of Mackinaw.

Tough Week For The S.T Atwater

The prospects for a good shipping season along the Saginaw River looked bright in the first days of April, 1886. It was nearly 40 years before the automobile and industrial boom on the Great Lakes; the business now was the production of lumber. Mills along the Saginaw river had steamed away throughout the long winter to stockpile enough of it to keep the river busy all season. In their mansions along the river, the fat lumber-barons puffed on giant cigars and gazed out into the gray April days, pondering the money they would make in the months ahead. Thirty days later, on the first of May, the ice had gone from the river, the sky had turned from gray to blue and the bottom had fallen out of the lumber-baron's fantasies.

Long-shoremen in both Saginaw and South Saginaw had been on strike. Even with the settling of the strike on the 2nd of May, there remained a great deal of agitation between the Long-shoremen in Saginaw and the rival Steveadores in Bay City who had refused to join the strike. To compound problems, the price of lumber cargoes had become depressed. Many of the wooden lumber hookers which had laid up in the river for the winter remained tied up and idle. Others simply sat near the docks with black coalsmoke trickling from their stacks as their masters waited for a price that would make a passage worthwhile. On the docks sat an estimated three hundred million feet of lumber and the owners had stated flatly that they were in no hurry to ship it at the current depressed prices. As if to add to all this competition, during the day of May 2nd the propeller Porter Chamberlain arrived towing the barges Mary Birkhead, Alice B. Norris, and Henry W.Hoag. The steambarges Germania, Glasgow and P.H. Birkhead also snored into the river on that spring Monday. Topping off the day's arrivals came the schooner Manzanilla, the barges W.W. Stewart, B.W. Jenness, C.N. Ryan, Myron Butman and City of the Straits. All of these boats waiting to open their holds to the market forcing the lumber rates farther down. Looking across the forest of masts, and considering that more boats were on the way, it was easy to see that this was going to be a tough week for the lumber fleet.

One small lumber boat was to have more than her fair share of trouble in the days ahead. The tiny lumber barge S.T. Atwater was in tow of the steambarge Alpena, upbound in Lake Huron. Off of Lexington, Michigan a dull thud shook the Atwater and the small boat's wooden hull began to leak. A sunken cake of ice had been lurking deep below Lake Huron's surface and the S.T. Atwater's hull was to be its victim.

After being signalled of the lumber barge's distress, the Alpena slowed to a stop and tucked the Atwater up near her. The barge was taking on a good deal of water, so much in fact, that that some of the Alpena's crew had to be put aboard to contain the flooding. For hours the men worked until the Atwater was out of danger. When it was determined that the Atwater would require drydocking in order to be repaired, the tug George B Dickson was dispatched to tow the lumber barge to Bay City. The Alpena continued on her way up the Lakes, minus her consort and several crewmembers.

The sun was just setting on this fine May evening in Bay City. Shops were closing and the heads of countless households were paying their daily penny for a copy of the Bay City Tribune to read at home that evening. The boat men would take special notice of latest the marine news. May 3rd's news included the arrival of the schooner Manzanilla and the barge Charles H. Davis over the past two days. Also, there was the account of the schooner Frank C. Leighton being damaged by a collision with the schooner Mineral State. The two were in tow of the tug Peter Smith and entering Lake Huron when the Leighton struck a cake of submerged ice and came to a dead stop. The Mineral State, which was second in tow, had no choice but to run up the Leighton's stern. Perhaps it was this same ice which had bitten into the S.T. Atwater, who on this calm spring evening came sluggishly into Bay City, smothered in the black smoke of the tug Dickson.

It had been a nasty bit of luck that landed the Atwater in the Saginaw River. The boat was put quickly into the Bay City drydock and the following morning the boatyard gang began the process of replacing white oak timbers and recaulking sprung seams. They were casual experts at what is today a lost craft. The workmen went about the task of repairing the S.T. Atwater as routinely as today's aircraft mechanics go about servicing a modern jet, unaware that a century later their profession would no longer exist.

While the Atwater was in drydock her master and mate had not been idle. They had been riding the trollies and pounding the red-bricked streets of east and west Bay City. Their objective was to muster a profitable cargo for the barge to carry out of Bay City, making up for the loss of this unexpected side trip. Resourceful were the men who could extract a profitable cargo out of a marketplace as depressed as the Saginaw riverfront was in those first days of May, 1886. It was arranged that the Atwater would carry a cargo of barreled vinegar and barreled cement for Tondawanda, New York when she was floated free of the Bay City drydock.

On May 6th, 1886, the tug Dickson, which had brought the Atwater into the Saginaw river in a leaking condition two days before, now took her back in tow on the short hawser and headed up into the Saginaw River. On board the Atwater her crew breathed a sigh of relief at finally getting their vessel out of the boatyard and back to work. Ahead of the Dickson and Atwater the tug Cheney was also headed up with the wooden barge Superior in tow. This combination of tug and wooden lumber barge was a very common sight on the River and Bay before the turn of the century. Another common sight was the tug and log-raft combination. Upbound ahead of the two tugs and barges on the evening of May 6, 1886, were the tiny tugs James

Hay and Jordan Beebe Jr, each with a giant raft of logs on their way to Saginaw's saw mills.

As this small wooden flotilla approached the Second Street bridge inbound, the tugs Avery and Sarah Smith, each with a raft of logs in tow, were approaching the Third Street bridge in the opposite direction less than a mile ahead. As if to add to the traffic the ferryboat Hall was making a landing between the two bridges.

Dense river traffic such as this flowed daily in the lumber era with little trouble, but today a hitch would develop. As the Beebe and Hay slipped through the Second Street swing-bridge, the Beebe cleared the west draw and beside her the Hay chugged through the east draw. Half a mile behind the tugs and rafts came the Cheney and Superior, followed closely by the Dickenson and the luckless S.T. Atwater. At 5:30 p.m. the Beebe and Hay went to pass through the Third Street bridge. The Beebe again taking the west draw and the Hay taking the east. This time the Hay's raft fouled in the bridge pier and stuck fast.

A traffic-jam had begun and all the boats approaching Bay City's Second and Third Street bridges had little choice other than to play a part in it. The Smith and Avery checked down short of Third Street to allow the Beebe to pass and wait for the Hay to clear her raft. Meanwhile the Cheney and Superior checked down in the Second Street east draw and the Dickson, not wanting to involve the poor S.T. Atwater in further trouble, slowed as much as the current would allow in the west draw.

Onboard the tug James Hay, two crewmen jumped onto the raft. The tug backed as the two lumbermen worked feverishly to clear the raft from the Third Street draw. The itchy tug captains were not to be delayed by this blockade. As the Beebe made it up through the Third Street draw, the tug Avery and her raft of logs scooted past in the opposite direction. No sooner had these two tugs cleared the bridge then the Cheney rang "ahead" and with the barge Superior squeezed past the Avery and into the draw.

Onboard the Dickson and Atwater, the crews had been watching with a note of amusement. After all, their boat was stopped safely inside the Second Street draw, far from where the Hay was now struggling to free her log raft and well clear of the clamor of tugs, rafts, and barges currently bottle-necked between the two bridges. Soon the hooting of signals and the shouting of curse words came to an end and it appeared to the Dickson that it was clear to pull the Atwater on through the Third Street bridge. With a billow of black smoke and a hiss of white steam the tug and barge moved forward.

While cutting over to the west draw the Dickson and Atwater passed the ferry boat Hall which was still attempting to make a landing. Without warning, the stern of the ferry boat swung out into the channel. A crunching jolt shook the S.T. Atwater as the Hall struck her astern. The Atwater's people watched helplessly as their boat was forced into the Third Street pier. The planks in the barge's bow caved in and damage was also done to her stern. It was back to the boat-yard for the Atwater less than two hours after she had left it.

On Saturday, May 8, the Dickson pulled the S.T. Atwater clear of the Saginaw river, nearly a full week after Lake Huron's ice had diverted her there. With a belly filled with barreled cement and vinegar consigned to Tondawanda, the tired old barge was pulled silently across the open bay. Perhaps the boat and crew breathed a sigh of relief, after all it had been a tough week for the S.T. Atwater.

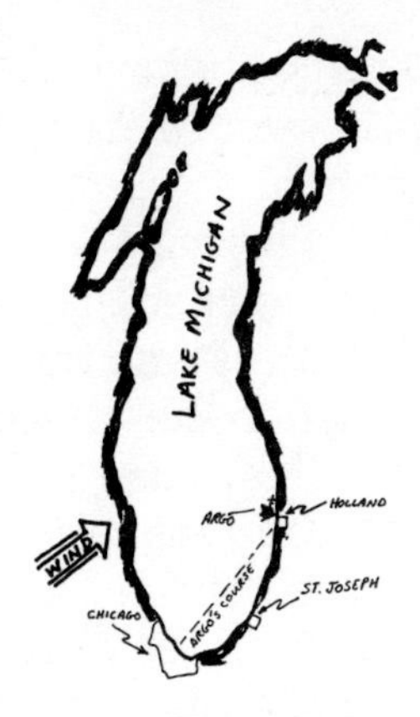

The Argo And Her Master

On the stormy evening of November 23, 1905, Isaac Newton's law of inertia was the farthest thing from Captain John Stewart's mind as he gazed out the pilothouse window of Graham & Morton Company's passenger steamer Argo. It is more likely that the good captain was reminiscing about cozy winter nights gone by at his Bay City home. Perhaps breeze filled summer visits to Bay City and the welcome the town's residents gave the well-known captain were the images projected in his mind as he peered into the darkness of the company's Chicago dock. In any case, the law of physics which states that an object will remain at a constant velocity in a straight line unless acted upon by an unbalanced outside force was definitely not a subject for the captain's pondering. This simple law of inertia would be applied without mercy to the steamer Argo before the night was over and Captain Stewart would be given a sudden lesson in the laws of physics.

Below near the gangway purser J.E. Hall of Mantowak,Wisconsin was checking in the boat's 25 passengers. George Bennett was far from his Fargo, North Dakota home when he checked aboard the Argo that night. Purser Hall also neatly printed the names T.F. Brown, P. Endress, and L.O.Decamp on his list of passengers. All three were from the tiny town of Ionia, Michigan and were together on a business adventure to the big city of Chicago. Also on the purser's list was the name H. Brown of Grand Rapids, Michigan and next to his name the note "colored" was added. This was a common practice for segregative distinction in 1905. Even though today such an action would draw outrage from all circles, it was just the way things were done everywhere in 1905. Using your imagination, it is not difficult to picture what kind of accommodations Mr. H.Brown "colored" had on his trip from Chicago to Holland, Michigan that night.

A healthy west-southwest wind was blowing as the Argo entered open Lake Michigan and a good sized chop had formed. These late November storms were nothing new to Captain Stewart. He had become old friends with the Lakes and their storms while sailing on the old steamer Metropolis and the steamer Arundel of the the shore line fleet. He had also commanded the steamer Dove before taking charge of the Argo's pilothouse. During his career as a master of vessels, Captain Stewart had developed a reputation as a cautious and cool headed pilot. Often when Lake Michigan had flared its temper, he had elected to take the Argo into St. Joseph Harbor rather than attempt the treacherous

Holland Harbor entrance. He knew all too well that the entrance at Holland had claimed many vessels in the past. The story always seemed to be the same, in fact only two years before the steamer Soo City had been molested by it . Shifting sands would shoal the channel and after striking the shoal the vessel loses headway and is swept against that deadly north breakwall. After being beaten there, the now helpless boat is pushed north into the sandbars and surf to be put to death. Yes, Captain Stewart kept that north breakwall in mind as did every vessel master who used the Holland Harbor. Even on the calm days of summer, each captain would steam past the north breakwall eyeing it with the contempt of a prize fighter passing his opponent on the way to the arena.

Halfway across Lake Michigan, the winds shifted slightly to the southwest, but intensified in strength to 55 miles per hour. The Argo was now beginning to take a heavy sea on the starboard stern quarter. The boat began to cork-screw in the following sea. There was no snow or rain, just the ice cold wind shrieking through the rigging. This weather would not make the night's passage one bit comfortable for the passengers of the Argo, but it would at least speed the boat's progress to the Michigan shore.

Just before 4:00 a.m.the lights of the Holland channel entrance came into view and Captain Stewart lined the Argo up with the channel. The boat continued to roll heavily but lined up very well despite the wind and waves. Soon the Argo was nearing the entrance lights. With the dip of a giant rolling wave, every person and object on the Argo jolted forward. In an instant every slug of forward inertia that had been earned by the Argo had been expended. Sir Isaac Newton's law had just bankrupted the *Argo* of all the forward energy she had accumulated on her way across Lake Michigan and she would have to open a new account.

Captain Stewart grabbed the pilothouse rail. "No," he growled to himself, knowing in an instant what had happened. A second wave brought another shudder and the stern of the *Argo* began to sweep to port. Captain Stewart rang full ahead and ordered the wheel hard to port. The wheelsman reached to the bottom of the wheel and grabbing the lowest pin flung it over as if to toss the whole apparatus out the pilothouse window. It was too late. The *Argo* could not gain enough forward way in time to save her from the rocky teeth of the north breakwall.

For minutes that felt like hours, the *Argo* fought a losing battle to gain her way and right herself in the channel. Then came the sickening grind of a tortured hull pounded onto rocks. Again, every object that was not firmly affixed to the boat jolted, but this time to port. Lake Michigan had impaled the *Argo* on the outermost tip of Holland Harbor's north breakwall. For a few moments, the steamer sat motionless tilted on the breakwall, but the big lake was not finished with her. With another low groan the now helpless *Argo* began to pivot toward the open lake. A series of waves crashed against her bow and the boat was pushed from the breakwall. The wind and waves now began to work the boat north toward the sandbars off the beach. Even at full ahead power, the *Argo* remained unable to gain headway against the storm. After drifting 1800 feet north, the *Argo* again shoaled some 200 feet off the beach.

In the Holland Lifesaving Station the alarm bell summoned the lifesavers. The lights of the *Argo* could be seen clearly through the spray, but when the rolling of the masthead lights turned into a twisting heave, the lifesavers wasted no time in gathering on the beach. There near the shore, the Argo teetered, rolling with each breaking wave and threatening to go to pieces with each crash of surf. If she were to do so, there was the very real possibility that none of the 36 souls aboard the steamer could survive a swim to shore in the storm churned ice water.

Shortly before 5:30 on that stormy morning the men of the Holland Lifesaving Station were preparing to rig a breeches buoy from the beach to the rolling Argo. This combination of ropes, pulleys and a sling-seat has been used to rescue shipwrecked sailors countless times. A line is shot by a mortar to the distressed boat and from that the ropes and pulleys are rigged. The chair is then wheeled to and from the boat to transfer those onboard.

From the beach the lifesavers took careful aim at the Argo. The first line fired was a complete miss. Most of the passengers and crew of the steamer had gathered on deck to watch the rescue attempt, and each breaking wave that struck the boat showered its helpless occupants with stinging cold spray. On the beach, the lifesavers hurriedly recovered the rescue line and carefully prepared for another shot. The lives of 36 people depended on their frozen hands.

The storm continued to rage, and through the spray and wind, a second shot was fired. This time the thin line was a direct hit and lodged firmly in one of the steel boat's fenders. A score of hands grabbed for the line as if grasping for hope itself. Using the small thin line, the Argo's people tugged the heavier breeches buoy rigging aboard the steamer. Remarkably, not one person on the stricken boat knew how to properly rig the buoy. They struggled for nearly an hour, but it soon became obvious to those ashore that something more had to be done.

Daylight found most of the residents of Holland, Michigan gathered at the lake shore braving the freezing cold wind and spray to watch the drama of the Argo unfold. Captain Poole of the United States Life Saving Service at Holland had formulated a plan and presented it to his group of lifesavers also gathered on the beach. Robert Vos, William Waldering, Francis Cady, Robert Smith, Harry Vandenberg, John Roberts, and Oscar Johnson listened intently to their captain's scheme. It was a plan of desperation, but with the storm not letting up and the Argo rolling on the shoal as if to go to pieces at any time, desperate steps were needed. The lifesavers would row out through the breaking frigid waves and try to put one of their own men aboard the teetering steamer. This meant three things: first there was the very real possibility that the tiny surf boat would be swamped on the way out resulting in the loss of everyone aboard; second, should the steamer break-up, the man put aboard would obviously suffer the same fate as her passengers and crew; and last of all, the man who manipulates the breeches buoy would more than likely be the last man off the boat. The task would require a volunteer.

No sooner had Captain Poole uttered the word volunteer than Robert Smith took two steps boldly forward, planting his feet firmly in the cold beach sand. He turned a cocky gaze defiantly toward the raging Lake. Before the other lifesavers has a chance to offer themselves, Captain Poole had found his volunteer.

Aboard the Argo, Captain Stewart was taking desperate steps of his own to aid in keeping his vessel from coming apart. He ordered water to be pumped aboard the boat in order to settle her firmly onto the bottom. Once resting on solid ground the big steamer would no longer be rocking on the shoal and would probably be less apt to twist herself apart in the pounding waves. There was no panic or commotion aboard the Argo. Captain Stewart, being a calm, collected master of vessels, had displayed a cool control that had spread among the Argo's crew and passengers. All of those now marooned aboard the fetched-up steamer simply gathered on the boat's rail to watch the effort that would decide their fate. Down in the engine room the fire gang was able to keep up steam, so the vessel had heat to all areas. As long as she held together, her people would at least not freeze.

Robert Smith along with four other lifesavers pushed the small surf boat into the breaking waves. Each crest that broke over the open boat drenched the plucky lifesavers with stinging cold water. It took only moments for hands pulling at wooden oars to become numb. The crowds both on the wind ripped beach and the stricken Argo held their breath each time the little boat would punch the crest of a wave and plunge from sight down the other side. Constantly being swamped by the frothing surf, the pint-sized rescue-boat was nearly lost a dozen times as it wallowed out to the steamer. The problem now would be getting Robert Smith from the tossing surfboat to the rolling deck of the Argo, nearly 20 feet from the surface of the lake. This would not be an easy task considering that if the small wooden boat drew too near it may be smashed into toothpicks against the big steamer's steel hull.

With a skill befitting the fine tradition of the United States Lifesaving Service, the tiny surfboat was drawn within range of the moaning steamer. A rope cast from the Argo's deck plopped across the rescue-boat. Oars fell loose as ten frozen hands grope,~ for the slithering line. Quickly nabbing the soaking rope, Robert Smith pulled it taut. Winding it once around his chest and twice around his left arm, he sprung from the surfboat. Swinging like a bob on a string, slapping against the solid hull of the big steamboat, and severely spraining his ankle. At the other end of the rope, desperate men hauled hand-over-hand to hoist Smith to the Argo's deck. Painful moments later, he tumbled safely over the boat's rail to the cheers of all those involved. Then a sharp snap like a cannon shot resounded from behind the crowd gathered on the stranded Argo. The spar to which the breeches buoy had been attached snapped and the life-line that connected the Argo to dry land began to tumble overboard. The crowd on the beach gasped as they watched what could be the last hope for the Argo's people fall toward the lake. Crew members and passengers alike leaped toward the retreating line. A death grip hold was put upon the wayward rope as a half dozen people piled onto it. Again secure, the line was now held fast by the desperate hands of the Argo's passengers.

Limping to the top of the Argo's deckhouse, Robert Smith re-rigged the breeches buoy line. This time the device was workable and he signaled to the lifesavers on shore to send over the chair. Squeaking and bouncing, the breeches buoy seat swung just above the crests of the frigid white-caps. Nearly ten minutes were used to get the empty breeches buoy to the deck of the Argo. The order of rescue would be women and children first. Captain Stewart glanced around the deck toward the shivering crowd. His gaze quickly fell upon Mrs. C.E. Johnson. He signaled to her indicating that she would be the first to make the trip to shore. Not wanting to be the first person to make the perilous trip through the maelstrom of frozen spray and icy water, Mrs. Johnson shrunk back into the crowd.

A plucky woman from Chicago, Mrs. P.J. Niskern, stepped boldly forward. She would be the first to attempt to make shore, testing the breeches buoy rig for the others. The seat swung wildly as it cleared the Argo, nearly dumping her out the side. As the breeches buoy was tugged farther away from the steamer, it sagged nearer to the roaring lake. The wind continued to howl and tossed the buoy seat about as if it were a paper toy. Long before the rig was close to halfway to shore, it was dipped into the first icy wave. When the frigid water slapped into Mrs. Niskern and the breeches buoy, it took her breath away and caused every muscle in her body to quake uncontrollably. After this soaking dip, the seat sprung up between the waves to be again exposed to the stinging wind.

From shore the crowd watched without a word as the breeches buoy rig was hauled slowly toward the shore being dipped from sight countless times. Repeatedly the tiny chair and the shivering woman who clung to it were dipped into the frothing maelstrom. After what felt like an hour, Mrs. Niskern reached the (dry sand of the Holland beach. The safe arms of the Holland lifesavers, warm spirits, and a dry wool blanket were there to greet her. She had proven to the people aboard the stricken Argo that the fragile rig could save their lives. The remaining two women and one twelve year old girl were loaded one at a time to make the soaking 200 foot journey to dry land.

The male passengers were next in line and soon the total passengers safely shivering on the beach numbered nine. As the seat was being reeled back out toward the Argo its line fell into the agitated lake. The lines to the boat had parted and the entire process of rescue would have to start again. It was just after 11:30 in the morning when the rescue lines broke and the storm began to blow harder. Lake Michigan seemed to want the captain from Bay City and his boat as badly as he wanted to foil its efforts. As the rampaging lake gathered its might, Captain Stewart remained calm and collected. Even when the lifeline to shore fell away, there was no panic. Captain Stewart's calming confidence had influenced all of the Argo's people to the point where the big lake could not terrify them.

Again the lifesavers took to their surfboat to float another breeches buoy line out to the Argo. This time the lake beat them back before they had gotten 50 feet out into the surf. A second try was also defeated by Lake Michigan. Soaked, frozen, and discouraged , the four lifesavers dragged their water filled surfboat onto the beach. The gale had reached its peak with the wind now screaming over the Argo at nearly 60 miles per hour.

Those on shore watched helplessly for nearly two hours as the storm raked over the big passenger steamer. Suddenly just before two o'clock in the afternoon, the wind died to the point where a line could again be shot out to the Argo. This time the first shot was on target and the breeches buoy was quickly re-rigged.

One by one, the passengers of the Argo made the dangling, wet, cold trip to the beach. Calm still prevailed as the storm began to die. The big steamer had now settled firmly on the sandy bottom, filled with the water that Captain Stewart had been pumping in for just that reason. Although listed over at greater than a 45 degree angle the boat was no longer shifting and was now in little danger of breaking up. So confident was the Bay City captain, that he and a handful of his crew remained on the Argo through the night.

It was the warmth of the Holland Lifesaving Station that stopped the shivering of the Argo's soaked people. Lake Michigan had been cheated out of 36 lives and the following spring the Argo herself would be raised from the lake's icy clutches to sail again. While walking along the tilted deck of his charge, Captain Stewart knew that the lake had put him out of a job at least for the rest of the 1905 season. At worst, the big lake had put him in the position that every vessel master dreads, that of having to explain in detail to the vessel owners why their boat was not currently in a position to earn money for them. At best, his coolheaded guidance had saved his boat from going to pieces and prevented panic among those shipwrecked with him.

Later that evening, the Argo's passengers could be found making their ways toward their final destinations. Aside from a good soaking and a sneeze or two they were unscratched. In fact, the only injury belonged to Robert Smith who spent the evening basking in a well deserved hero's spotlight...one foot soaking in a large bucket of ice water.

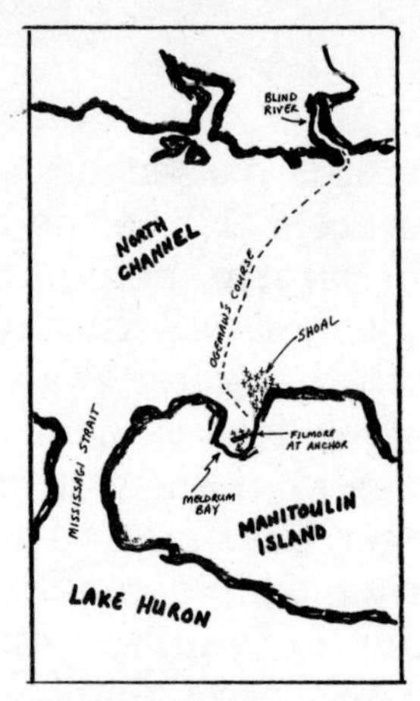

Against The Odds

For seven months of each year the waters of the Great Lakes are free of winter ice. During this time hundreds of lakeboats pound their way along the designated lanes of shipping. Even in modern times, when the number of lakers has been decreased to a few hundred, it is not uncommon for the boatwatcher standing on Lake Huron's shore to see a string of longships on the horizon. In 1913 the number of boats steaming along the Lakes was more than four-fold that of today. Like ants on a sidewalk following an invisible trail from food to nest, the boats would push silently past one another. Upbound and downbound, heavy and light, the steady parade of long steel freighters, canallers, whalebacks, lumber hookers, barges, and schooners continued, 24 hours a day until the winter ice again forced them to stop.

On the seventh day of November, 1913, the

most powerful storm in Great Lakes history began to sweep across all of the freshwater seas. In this era, vessel masters often ignored weather and commonly pushed their boats into violent storms in lieu of losing a day of gainful hauling' while waiting for more favorable conditions. Also this was an age when weather prediction was basically non-existent, you knew what the weather was going to be when it happened. As a result scores of boats were caught out on the open lakes and savagely assaulted by the 1913 storm. Other boats sailed from the protection of ports and rivers directly into the building maelstrom. Once into the heaving lake and shrieking wind the boats had no choice other than running before the wind, or making a desperate charge toward any kind of shelter. That once orderly parade of vessels turned into a confusion of individual boats tossed about the Lake.

Five days later, the storm died and a dozen boats had been swallowed by the freshwater. Over two dozen had been blown ashore. Six of these were never to sail again. Because of the inaccurate records kept in those days, the exact number of sailors killed will never be known. It was common practice in this era to hire on unskilled crewman for as little time as a single trip. Many of these men were little more than vagrants who could coil a rope or swing a coal shovel. These men were consumed by the Lakes and will never be missed or accounted for. Estimates of the lives lost range from 250 to over 300. More than 50 human existences were blotted out anonymously. Giant steel freighters considered to be unsinkable by weather were wiped from existence in the blink of an eye.

In light of these circumstances the odds were definitely against a pair of leaking old wooden lakeboats. But, on Saturday evening, November 8, 1913, the last thing Captain W.E. Pierce of the lumber hooker Ogemaw expected from Mother Nature was the deadliest storm in Great Lakes history. Bound for Cleveland from Blind River, Ontario, the Ogemaw had the schooner barge C.A. Filmore in tow. Both boats were bearing cargoes of fresh Canadian lumber from the north shore of Lake Huron's Georgian Bay. It was under the responsibility of the E.B. Foss Lumber Company that the nearly one million board feet of lumber would be transported.

Launched at St. Clair, Michigan, in 1881, the Ogemaw measured 162 and one half feet in length. She had a beam of 30 feet and a depth of just over 11 feet. The C.A. Filmore was constructed at Bay City's F.W. Wheeler Yard in 1889. Normally the 161 foot Filmore was towed by the Foss steamer Benton, but in 1904 she became the steady consort of the Ogemaw. By the 1913 season the two boats were in their golden years by wooden boat standards.

A westwind with a fair bite to it was whipping across the north channel of Georgian Bay as the Ogemaw pulled the Filmore from Blind River. Less than an hour out, the wind shifted suddenly to the north, northeast and blasted across both vessels. The calm Indian summer night turned to thick cold darkness, and the seas rose in a terrifyingly short time. In 40 years of sailing on the Lakes, Captain Pierce had never seen the fresh waters become so quickly angered.

From the blackness of the night the wild lake came to torture the two lumber boats. Wave after wave came aboard to pluck away at their cargoes of lumber. Slapping against the stern of each boat the water began to ship aboard. On the Filmore cabin doors were burst in, windows aft shattered, and her cargo hold began to flood. Forward, water burst beneath the companionway door and loose articles were sloshing about on the floor. Layer by layer the schooner's neatly stacked lumber cargo washed away.

Pounding ahead of the rolling Filmore, the Ogemaw was also being savagely mauled. The bow of the tiny steamer was repeatedly slammed into the rolling sea. Her screw was pulled high out of the water as the crest of each wave rolled under her midship. The wind ripped the crest from the seas and pelted the old boat without mercy. Between the two boats the thick towing hawser stretched tight like iron bar, the peaks of the seas at times swallowing nearly its length.

After only five and a half hours of this punishment Captain Pierce felt that the end of either his vessel or his consort was inevitable. Passing through Mississagi Straits in this weather would be impossible, and once on the raging, open Lake Huron, both boats would be easy prey. Turning back toward the lee of north shore with the barge in tow was out of the question. Meldrum Bay however, was only a couple of points to the east. Even though the mouth of the Bay opens to the north it still offers a very modest shelter from a northeaster. The saying," any ol' port in a storm," was applicable in this situation. Captain Pierce hauled for the Bay, and if his boat didn't sink before he got there, Captain Pierce and his 16 man crew as well as the 8 man crew of the Filmore might just live to see Sunday morning.

Rolling madly the Ogemaw and her schooner-barge consort headed into Meldrum Bay. Getting into its shelter would require a fair bit of seamanship in good weather, but in the pitch black of night during the Great Storm of 1913, making Meldrum Bay would be just short of a miracle. Captain Pierce would be forced to angle to the west close to the west shore to avoid the rocky shoal that bottlenecks the mouth of the Bay. Then if the gale force wind didn't blow the boats onto the western shore, he would have to turn nearly 90 degrees to round below the shoal and tuck up as close as possible to the Bay's east shore.

Navigating nearly blind the Ogemaw's master used every day of his 40 years experience to snake the vessels into Meldrum Bay. Once out of the giant seas, only the wind remained to beat upon the boats. Pulling the steamer's bow as close as he dared to the east shore Captain Pierce dropped the boat's big anchors. Checking his engine down to "slow ahead" Captain Pierce let the wind catch the Filmore, swinging both boats around to head the storm. The schoonerbarge then tossed both of her big hooks over the side, the plan now was to wait out the storm.

By late Sunday night the worst gale in Great Lakes history had intensified. Now the screaming wind brought sleet mixed with thick snow. The Ogemaw's master had been steadily increasing the boat's engine revolutions from "slow ahead" to "full ahead" in order to keep her anchors from dragging. A wind made of iron however was more than the anchors of the steamer could tolerate, they lost their hold and began to slip from Meldrum Bay's rocky bottom. Captain Pierce knew that the storm was blowing the old lumber hooker toward the south shore, there to be dashed to pieces by the surf. The condition of the C.A. Filmore could not be seen through the blowing ice, snow, and the deep black night. It was easy to figure that her situation was little better than the Ogemaw's. Besides with the old schooner-barge still tethered to the Ogemaw's stern, the steamer could not maneuver at all. The only choice that the Ogemaw's master could make in order to save his boat was to cut the barge loose and run for wide open water. Leaving the Filmore to her own ends, the steamer pushed out into the insanity of the storm tossed Georgian Bay.

A run for the Blind River would be the only hope for the Ogemaw and her 16 men. Once on the open water the boat was exposed to the storm's fury. Waves towering six feet over the tiny steamer's pilothouse slammed down onto her. Foaming swirling ice water engulfed the little boat. Aft of the pilothouse, the windows of the first mate and captain's quarters were smashed in by the booming waves. Shortly after that, the walls of the deckhouse itself began to buckle and then, piece by piece the whole structure was carried away by the raging waves. Within what remained of the Ogemaw's pilothouse, a drenched Captain Pierce felt that his boat was doomed. Taking to the lifeboats was out of the question under the present conditions, getting to them would be suicide, and launching them among this madness would be impossible. Certainly the Ogemaw would go to the bottom with all hands at any moment.

Perhaps the boat builders at St. Clair, Michigan had put a tad more elbow grease into the Ogemaw's planking, or maybe her oak timbers had come from trees with just a bit more spring to them, in any case shortly after daylight, Captain Pierce peered through the boat's broken pilothouse window at the Blind River entrance. By lunchtime, the

Ogemaw's 16 shaken crewman were drying out what remained of their possessions and figuring out ways to cobble repairs on what remained of their boat which was now tied snugly to the dock from where it had departed. For the next 24 hours, the Ogemaw waited for the open water to settle down enough to allow safe passage to Meldrum Bay where the Filmore had been left. On Tuesday afternoon, the steamer, minus her forward deckhouse and officer's quarters, put out to recover what remained of her barge. Surely by now she had been pushed ashore and dashed to pieces on the rocks, or overcome by the wind and waves and swept from existence. There was always the chance that some of her crew may have reached the hostile Meldrum Bay shore. At the very least, the Ogemaw may rescue a few shipwrecked sailors.

Three hours out of Blind River, the Ogemaw rolled again into Meldrum Bay. To the surprise of everyone onboard, the ice-coated hull of the Filmore was anchored firmly where they had left her nearly two days before. The majority of her cargo of lath had been carried away by the storm, but the appearance of her crew on deck told everyone onboard the Ogemaw that the Filmore had come through the worst storm in history with hardly a scratch.

With her consort again safely in tow, the Ogemaw pushed out of Meldrum Bay and headed for Mississagi Strait, five miles to the west. Once through the narrow pass the two boats headed due south into an open Lake Huron. It was there that the Ogemaw and Filmore found the big lake to be still enraged by the storm. Waves over 15 feet pounded both boats, and an Arctic cold wind blew thick snow flurries. It wasn't until ten o'clock on

Wednesday morning that the two lumber boats made the safety of Alpena's harbor. Each boat was sporting a 12 inch coating of ice on her hull from the passage across the open lake.

Weeks later the death toll had been added up, and most of the lakeside communities had started to recover from the shock of the Great Storm. E.B. Foss had commissioned repair work on his two boats, Ogemaw and C.A. Filmore. Captain Pierce was set to spend the winter spinning yarns about his brush with doom, and although neither he nor Mr. Foss came right out and boasted it publicly, both knew that the Foss boats had beaten the odds.

Without the benefit of modern weather forecasting, Captain W. E. Pierce took the **Ogemaw** and her barge **C. A. Filmore** into the worst storm in Great Lakes history.

Courtesy of Milwaukee Public Library

Judge Tuttle's Letter

Over the years, much has been made of the survivors of the Great Storm of 1913. Boats such as the J. H. Sheadle and the Howard M. Hanna Jr. were chewed upon by that devastating storm, yet lived to sail on for many decades after. Historians and boat buffs alike have watched with a special sense of appreciation as these famous boats would steam by. There were, however, other giant lake freighters who survived those terrible days and worked on for many years without the fame of a Great Storm survivor. Most of these boats went on to be renamed, reconstructed, or converted. These older smaller boats would often live out their golden years working the rivers and back waters of the Great Lakes where their smaller size would allow them to navigate easily and earn a fair profit for their age. The Saginaw River would be the eventual work-place for such boats.

Throughout the 1960's and early 1970's, the 557 foot J. F. Schoellkopf Jr. would hiss quietly up and down the Saginaw River, largely unnoticed by those who live and work along its banks. The big steel steamer didn't wear any kind of tag saying "survivor", nor did she bear any other marks that would indicate that she had ever done anything other than steam passively up and down the murky waters of various rivers along the Great Lakes, delivering countless loads of assorted bulk cargos. She, in fact, wore the clever disguise of an over-enlarged wheelhouse, a self-unloading boom and an "A" frame support structure, and most deceptive of all, she sported a different name.

In mid November of 1913 the J. F. Schoellkopf was sailing in the long haul ore trade as the Hugh Kennedy. Her 557 foot size, at that time, was considered to be the working standard for that trade. If asked, her captain, Harvey A. Stewart, would probably have said there was little chance you would ever see his six year old boat making regular calls up the Saginaw River. After all, in 1913 the Saginaw River was the hub of what was then a declining lumber industry. The very thought of sailing a 550 foot class boat up that twisting, shoaling, shallow river with its multitude of narrow bridges would have seemed farfetched indeed. On Monday, the 17th of November, thoughts such as that were probably the farthest thing from Captain Stewart's mind when he sat down at his desk to pen a letter to his near relative, District Judge Arthur J. Tuttle. What was foremost on the mind of Captain Stewart was the violent raging storm that has just killed 250 to 300 of his brother sailors.

Several books and articles have been written

about the Great Storm of 1913, as well as detailed accounts of the weather patterns and the damage they did across the Great Lakes states. The full scope of the storm can be put into perspective here simply by noting that, in the Bay City, Michigan, area local businesses were closed for as long as five days after the storm.

Nearly two weeks after Bay City had dug out and patched up, Judge Arthur J. Tuttle made his way through the river town's red-brick streets. Most trolley service had been restored in full, but Judge Tuttle would still pass an occasional boarded window or unrepaired power line on his way to hold court. Hurricane force winds had brought snow that exploded like bird-shot down the narrow streets. Along the river every lumber hooker, schooner-barge, and tug made fast to their docks and put out extra lines.

On this cold November morning the honorable judge made his way through the few reminders of that deadly blow. Neatly folded in his pocket was the letter Captain Stewart had penned aboard the Hugh Kennedy accounting the boat's passage through the storm. Judge Tuttle was met at the courthouse by a plucky reporter from the Bay City Times. After a good deal of persuading the judge agreed to let the Bay City Times copy and print a portion of the letter that had been the talk of the town. The good judge had done a bit of boasting and the word was around that he had in his possession a juicy piece of inside information. The sound of crinkled paper echoed through the hallowed halls of the courthouse as the reporter eagerly unfolded the letter. Matting the letter down with one hand he tried to copy with the other. Only that part of the letter pertaining directly to the storm was allowed to be taken down, and it is with the permission of the same newspaper that it is reprinted here for the first time in over three quarters of a century.

"Steamer Kennedy, Monday Nov. 17, 1913

Dear Art:

"You said to write if I had time. Well, I have had time but I couldn't do it because that storm had kind of given me a shock. I can't see how it could happen and I have been at the business 24 years. Can you imagine how you would feel if 285 U. S. Judges should be wiped off the map quicker than the twinkle of an eye and you standing in the coop like the chicken looks that is left on Thanksgiving Day?

"I have always said no wind could blow that would wreck one of these boats, but I am obliged to say that the possibilities are that the reason I am here is because I was on Lake Superior and not on Huron. When I was on Lake Huron going up, my barometer was slowly dropping and when I got to White Fish Point it was going down fast with the wind blowing south about 40 or 50 miles an hour. This showed me that a storm was approaching from the west and would no doubt hit me in say twelve hours. So I stopped on the south shore for 65 miles. Then went across to the Point (Keweenaw). The wind died all the way to calm. That was the storm center.

"The barometer showed a storm was coming as far down as Alpena, Mich. Friday at 3:20 p.m. the storm hit me coming from the northeast. Then in an hour shifted to the north and blew about 86 miles an hour. We were forced to head into it and when I got to the north shore it was snowing hard and did so for about four hours.

"I arrived at Superior at 10:00 a.m. Saturday with the wind north at 40 miles an hour and the weather clear. I loaded Saturday. Barometer went up to nearly 30, showing cold but no doubt clear weather. I left Superior Sunday at 6:15 a.m. A nice day and no reports of any storm nor warning. When I left Superior there was no wind but I ran into it again at practically the same place I did on my way up trip.

"The wind blew about 60 miles an hour, I figure, and at puffs it may have gone to 65 or 70. It began to snow when we were off the west end of Isle Royal. It blew so hard that one could not hear the whistle blow and snowed awfully hard and ice froze onto us until we looked like an ice palace. A wire the size of your little finger was as large as a barrel. Can you imagine it?

"I wore a mackinaw with lumberman's pants and my clothes were frozen stiff. Just like a board. I caught no cold. Was up for three days and nights."

After passing downbound at the Soo, Captain Stewart guided the Hugh Kennedy into the still churning Lake Huron. Nineteen hours later the big steamer was literally pushing its way through the wreckage in Huron's southern "pocket." This included sailing past the overturned hull of the Charles S. Price. The timing for the Hugh Kennedy's survival could not have been better. The big boat caught the northern leading edge of the Great Storm on the way up. She was in port behind the storm loading all day Saturday while the winds and seas worked over the Peter White, Cornell, and Henry Cort. Captain Stewart sailed out into clear weather downbound behind the storm catching up to the worst of it at about the same time that the Henry B. Smith was being consumed. The Kennedy made her home-stretch run for Whitefish Bay and the Soo as Lake Huron was being polished off. Then down from the Soo toward the lower Lakes, there to tie-up safely as a survivor. It is said that each lakeboat develops a personality of its own and six decades after the great storm, the Hugh Kennedy would steam up and down the Saginaw River quiet and modest perhaps even shy to a fault. Her name having been changed to J. F. Schoellkopf Jr. helped her to hide her past. It always seemed that she did not display the fame of being a Great Storm escapee, but the nagging guilt of a survivor among fallen comrades.

Before she was sold to American Steamship Company in 1922 the **Hugh Kennedy** ran in Buffalo Steamship colors. It was under this flag that she was running when she found herself in the great storm of 1913.

Courtesy of The Great Lakes Historical Society

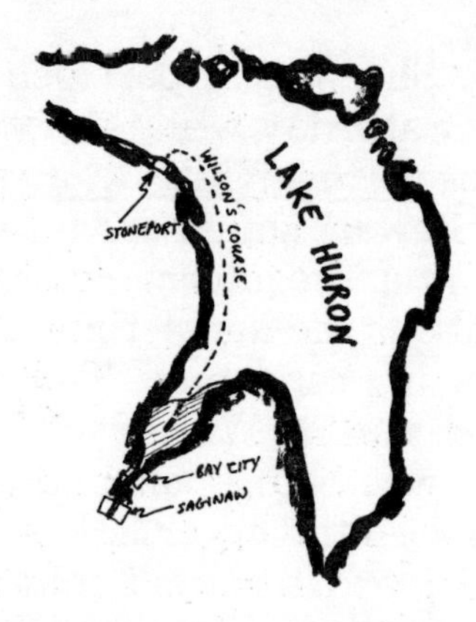

All In A Day's Frustration

The final days of any shipping season on the Great Lakes are a frustrating struggle between lake and lakeboat. Those who sail the lakes and the boats they sail upon handle these frustrations with a degree of patience that cannot be found elsewhere. A good example of this took place on a bitter cold weekend in December, 1985.

It was late on Thursday night, December 19, when American Steamship Company's big self-unloader, Charles E. Wilson, took the last rumbles of gravel through her hatches at Stoneport, Michigan. Located on the southern end of Presque Isle, Stoneport is one of the bustling hubs of Lake Huron's stone and gravel trade. Vessels often wait in line to take on any of the multiple grades of crushed rock mined in the giant open pits along the northeast shore of Michigan's lower peninsula. This portion of northern Lake Huron's vacation-land shoreline stands largely deserted by late December. The only activity that breaks the still of the frozen winter is the steady passage of the giant lakeboats. Countless tons of Michigan's bedrock is shuttled to dozens of ports around the Great Lakes. Five large mines serve as the primary source of cargo for the behemoth gravel carriers. At the northern end of Saginaw Bay is the port of Alabaster, named for the sparkling white rock that is prominent in its nearby pit mine. North along the east coast is the city of Alpena, home to the Huron Cement Company and the valuable gypsum used in making their powdered cement. A few miles farther north and tucked just below Presque Isle is Rockport, the southern-most of three sprawling pit mines located on and around the isle. Rogers City is at the northern tip of Presque Isle and is the primary port of call for the gray fleet of United States Steel's giant stone carriers. Between Rogers City and Rockport is the Stoneport facility. All along this portion of Michigan's lower peninsula, the industry is crushed rock in any quantity and any grade to fill any job. It would take a solid freeze of the lower lake ports to stop the steady parade of gravel carriers. On this day, the Charles E. Wilson was caught in the scurry of traffic attempting to meet tonnage commitments before the winter ice closed the lower lake ports.

The temperature hadn't risen above the teens anywhere on the Lakes for nearly two weeks and Stoneport was no exception. As a result, a respectable layer of ice had formed around the Wilson and far out into the lake. There was some question as to whether or not the big boat could get away from the dock at all, let alone sail all the way to the Wirt Stone Company's Belinda Street dock in

Bay City, Michigan, far down Lake Huron and into the Saginaw River. Getting there would require sailing into this twisting, winding, narrow waterway that has been a challenge to Great Lakes mariners for more than a century.

The Saginaw River is dotted for nearly its full length with bulk cargo docks such as the one to which the Wilson was now scheduled to unload. These docks are not the sprawling mechanized facilities that one would expect to be receiving daily boatloads of crushed rock. They are instead large clear areas roughly the size of a football field where a laker can swing her boom out and pyramid tall piles of cargo. Normally, a simple front-end loader then bites away at the giant heap. Dump-truck after dump-truck is filled until the dock is again clear and another lakeboat pushes silently up to expel its cargo. On this bitter cold December night the Bay City docks sat frozen, clear, and silent, waiting for the next load of stone to be piled where now only loose snow blew along the ground.

With a good deal of crunching and an equal amount of patience the Wilson broke away from the Stoneport dock and began to cram her way toward the open lake, leaving a path of giant crushed ice floating behind. No sooner had she cleared the piers than Algoma Central Railway's massive 730 foot self-unloader, Algosoo, took her place, a layer of ice forming around her hull shortly after the boat's lines were made secure. Aboard the Wilson the sharp cracking and the muffled crunch of breaking ice soon stopped as the boat entered the open cobalt blue water of upper Lake Huron. Once there, the Wilson and her crew went on with their work with very little fuss at all.

When she came out on September 9, of 1973,

the 680 foot Charles E. Wilson was one of the first of the "New Breed" of lakeboat. Gone are the traditional lines of beauty that were always built into lakeboats of the past, sacrificed in the name of efficiency. Also missing from this new breed are the forward wheelhouse and deckhouses. Usually planted atop their fo'c'sle is a telephone booth-like observation shelter. All of the deck houses are stacked on the stern. There are no curves of beauty here either. Everything is square, a squared pilot house, a square stack, and even square galley windows. No beauty contest would ever be won by the Wilson herself. Her coal-black hull resembles a 680 foot shoe box that is bluntly rounded on one end. Stacked on the aft end is a five story building-like structure. All crew accommodations are housed here in this white floating condominium. This structure is topped by a rectangular pilothouse that is mounted length-wise across it. Aft of her pilothouse is the rectangular smokestack which proudly bears the silver, red and silver horizontal stripes on a black background that are the mark of American Steamship Company. From the forward bottom of her deckhouses, a triangular truss supports the upper pivot for the boat's self-unloading boom. When locked in the stowed position, the boom rests upon the Wilson's spardeck and juts forward 250 feet. The boat is square, blunt, and just plain dull to look at. Bay Shipbuilding spared the dollar and spoiled the view when it produced this class of boat.

The Wilson may not be fun to look at, but American Steamship Company was not looking for a work of art to make their cargo runs; they wanted an efficient cargo carrying machine that could unload any bulk cargo nearly anywhere on the lakes.

It is in doing this that the Charles E Wilson comes into a realm of her own. From taconite to sand the big boat can haul a load of 23,000 tons to almost any dock within 200 feet of freshwater. There is no need for expensive shore-side unloading equipment. She simply pulls near the dock swings her boom out and delivers as much of her cargo as the customer needs, up to her capacity. This is one of the advantages that leads a smart company to invest in a Wilson class boat. Boats such as the Wilson are constructed quickly and, at just over 13 million dollars in cost, relatively inexpensively. The trade off is in aesthetics; after all, it costs money for oak paneling and tile showers. It takes time to scallop bowplates; squares are faster, inexpensive, and much more easily constructed.

The hull of a Wilson-class boat is also a departure from the standard lakeboat. Not since McDougal's whalebacks has such a radical departure been so widely accepted. The whalebacks which made their appearance in the early 1890s had spoonshaped bows and rounded sides. They gave the appearance of surfaced submarines when running loaded. The Wilson-class boat, with a squared off stern and round bluff bow, looks somewhat like half a popsicle stick with deckhouses. The Wilson's round bow would play an important part in this December's battle with the elements. This perhaps would be a good lesson for those who design boats; when you depart from the traditional norm you may find that "they used to do it that way" for a good reason.

Through the night, the Wilson and her crew went about their work routines with few problems and fewer complaints. As they approached Saginaw Bay, Captain John Allen took his place in the wheelhouse to guide his boat into and up the Saginaw River. Fully expecting to encounter some substantial ice, American Steamship Company had engaged the big ice-breaking tug *Gregory J. Busch* to break her way out into the bay to meet the *Wilson* and aid her in making her way through the icepacked river. At 150 dollars an hour, this was an expensive investment, but when compared with the *Wilson's* cost of over 500 dollars an hour, any investment in speeding her up river would be well worth the cost.

Unknown to Captain Allen of the *Charles E. Wilson*, these best laid plans were already beginning to go astray. As the tug *Busch* was breaking her way through Bay City, she came upon the big iron railroad bridge belonging to the Grand Trunk and Western. This giant black-iron monster spanned the Saginaw River with a series of truss structures. Before the turn of the century its span swung open as many as 50 times daily to let boats of the lumber fleets pass. Now, in 1985, the span was left in the open position during the river's busy season. Closing was done only to allow trains to cross. In its old age, the big iron bridge had gotten a bit crotchety and tended to stick in place, refusing to swing. Rather than holding up the busy summer season boat traffic for the convenience of an occasional train, the big swing span remained normally open. In mid-December the bridge's full-time position was changed to normally closed, opening only for the occasional late-season lakeboat. On this bitter December day, the black hulk of the old railroad bridge stood sulking silently across the frozen Saginaw River, as if making up its mind whether or not to go to work. The bridge tender stood in his control house poised to swing the

1800's vintage span open when the *Busch* blew her whistle. Slowing for the passage, the *Busch* blew the proper signal, the tender turned proper controls, and the bridge didn't move. Both parties repeated this process; the bridge refused to budge. Stopping 100 feet below the dark black trusses of the old bridge, the tug *Busch* began making radio calls. Via the Saginaw River Coast Guard, the bridge tender, who was without a radio, was contacted by landline. The bridge, he said, was stuck fast and there was nothing he could do. Next, the *Charles E. Wilson* was contacted on channel 16. Captain Allen decided to "keep 'er comin'"; after all, the *Wilson* was well able to handle most ice and the *Busch* was only to be an aid to her passage anyhow. Resigning himself to a somewhat slower passage he pushed his boat on into the Bay.

At daylight on Friday morning, a large field of ice appeared on the horizon ahead of the *Wilson*. Carefully, but firmly the *Wilson* pushed ahead into the sheet ice. With thunders of cracking and crunching, the pack of ice gave way until the big boat was well into its clutches. Then the boat's progress began to slow; her Loran-C over-the-bottom speed dropped until it read zero. The boat ground to a halt.

Backing his boat about one boat length the Captain rang forward, taking another stab at the ice. Once again some progress was made. Giant chunks of ice flew in all directions as the *Wilson* attacked the frozen surface of Saginaw Bay. About half a boat length was gained. The process was repeated over and over. Four hours later the *Charles E. Wilson* and her cargo of gravel had made four tenths of a mile in progress. She was up against windrows; the ice pushed by the wind had folded over upon itself doubling and tripling its strength. Some of these ridges were eight to twelve feet thick, more than a match for the rounded blunt bow of the Wilson.

What had started as a routine late season passage had now become a contest between modern technology and Mother Nature. When considering the elements and power that nature had on her side, the Charles E. Wilson was definitely the underdog. On her side, the big boat had only a skilled master and crew supported by modern technology and communications. There was also the Coast Guard and its fleet of ice-breaking vessels located around the Lakes. Mother Nature had on her side the Bay, the ice, the wind and time.

By mid afternoon, Captain Allen called the front office in Buffalo through the Bay City marine operator, to request assistance. The tug Busch was stuck behind the Grand Trunk bridge and the Wilson, if she continued at her present rate, would get into the river sometime next January. American Steamship Company quickly hired the icebreaking tug Barbara Ann, out of Port Huron to come to the aid of their big selfunloader, since the Coast Guard's icebreakers were committed to other vessels. The icebreaker Mackinaw was the closest to the scene, but she was at her home port of Cheboygan, Michigan, with only two of her four engines operating. Despite this handicap the Mackinaw cast-off her lines and proceeded down Lake Huron at a reduced speed of only nine and one half miles per hour. The trip to Saginaw Bay would now take twice as long, the Charles E. Wilson would have to wait.

Just after sunset it began to snow, in fact it soon became a blizzard. So heavy and sudden was the snow that the I-75 Expressway, which had been dry and clear at 6:00 p.m., was down to one lane moving at 35 miles per hour from Detroit to Mackinaw by 8:00 p.m. Out on Saginaw Bay the Wilson sat waiting surrounded by ice. Snowflakes the size of nickels swirled through the glow of the big boat's lights and gathered as small drifts in every open corner. Often the Wilson's bow could not be seen from her pilothouse. The wind became a stinging, numbing thing that seemed to hunt around the boat looking to freeze anything left exposed. Mother Nature was taking her turn at the Wilson tonight, and all the giant self-unloader could do was sit there like a bug in a web. It is a sure bet that being frozen in for the winter was not the subject of serious conversation onboard the Charles E. Wilson that night. That kind of thing has happened in decades past, but with today's giant ice breakers and modern communications, such a thing is nearly beyond possibility. The key word in the back of the minds of the Wilson's crew as they looked out into that thick choking snow was "Pressure." Ice in large quantities has an incredible amount of mass. It was, in fact, glacier ice that carved out the giant basins that are now the Great Lakes. Thick sheet ice, such as that now surrounding the Charles E. Wilson can shift in just the wrong way and crumple a hull like an aluminum beer can. To make matters worse, one of the worst places for shifting, unpredictable ice is Saginaw Bay, exactly where the Wilson was now stuck. Throughout the night and all of the following day each crunch and every groan, or creak that followed was met with uneasy boasts of confidence in the vessel by her crew.

Meanwhile, three miles inside the Saginaw

River, the icebreaking tug Gregory J. Busch was trying, without success, to convey to the Grand Trunk Railroad the significance of getting their stuck bridge opened. When speaking to Grand Trunk's regional superintendent, the tug Busch found him less than eager to get their bridge fixed. The crew of the Busch pointed out that just three days before they had experienced exactly the same problem while escorting the S.T. Crapo out of the river. The superintendent said he would try to get a repair gang out there the next day, but he couldn't promise anything, not even that the bridge would ever be open again.

It was clear and bitter cold the following night when masthead lights appeared on the northeast horizon. For hours they seemed not to move. Slowly, the tug Barbara Ann crushed her way to the Charles E. Wilson. Taking off the pressure would be the job of the Barbara Ann, and through the night she worked. Near dawn, the lights of the powerful icebreaker Mackinaw swung into sight. The Mackinaw pounded her way to, and past the Wilson. With the Mackinaw leading the way and the Barbara Ann at her side, the Wilson made forward progress for the first time in nearly two days.

Normally, this would be the end of a fairly frustrating chapter in the Charles E. Wilson's log, but now another problem developed caused by Mother Nature and complicated by the Wilson's round bow. A stiff, near gale force wind began to blow on Saginaw Bay. The Mackinaw would break a path ahead, but before the Wilson could follow, the ice would drift her to the east. There was now the very real threat that the deeply loaded boat could be pushed out of the narrow 25 foot deep channel into the surrounding bay where depths in many areas are only 18 feet and can get as low as only 5 feet. Should the boat be pushed aground out of the channel and if the ice were to anchor, making port until the spring would be a real possibility. This problem was compounded by the fact that the round bluff bow of the big self-unloader would not allow her to chip her way out of the path cut for her.

After a good deal of backing and re-cutting by the Mackinaw and with the near gale force wind letting up for only a few hours the Wilson's luck changed. The stubborn Grand Trunk Railroad bridge even groaned open to let the Gregory J. Busch pass. The tug began breaking her way out to meet the small fleet now working their way toward her in the opposite direction. Slowly, as if she had all the time in the world the big self-unloader pushed her way into the ice-choked Saginaw river. Thick sheetice like plateglass broke ahead of her round bow. Nearly two hours were consumed in the boat's passage into the winding river. Mother Nature had taken her shot at the big freighter and even if she were forced to move slowly, the wind and ice could not stop the powerful lakeboat again. Inching gingerly up to the Belinda Street dock Captain Allen's charge put out her lines, swung her boom over the bank and began unloading her cargo.

With the Wilson making her dock, the Mackinaw moved on to perform another routine rescue. The Barbara Ann tied up ahead of the Wilson. She would aid in turning the boat, and also would help the big lake boat on her outbound passage. When these tasks were finished the Barbara Ann would begin breaking her way back to port Huron with a fat payday on her book courtesy of Mother Nature and the Grand Trunk Bridge. It had been a long and frustrating passage for all those involved.

At the same moment as this story was coming to a close, Pringle Transit Company's 630 foot self-unloader William R. Roesch was breaking away from the exact same dock that the Charles E. Wilson had started from nearly four days before. The Roesch locked her boom in place and began crunching her way toward the open lake, her destination was the exact same dock where the Wilson was now piling her cargo of stone. And so it starts again.

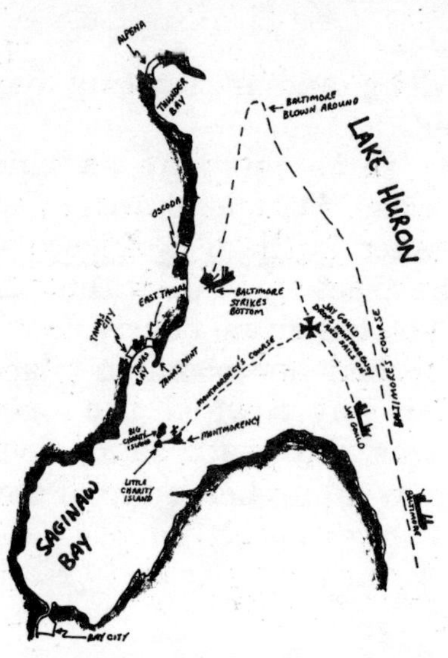

Every Man For Himself

Things were about as pleasant as they could be when the towline from the 160 foot schooner-barge James L. Ketchum plopped into the deep blue water of Saginaw Bay. Fall storms that so often churn the Lakes into a frenzy seemed far away on this fine Sunday evening. The schooner-barge Montmorency was being dropped off by the Ketchum and their towing steamer, the 235 foot Jay Gould, at the mouth of Saginaw Bay. This routine dispatch called for the Montmorency to raise her small sails and work her way toward the mouth of Saginaw River. Once there, one of the local steam tugs would come out and pull her in. As the Gould continued on down Lake Huron her mate dutifully noted the Montmorency's drop-off in the log, the date was May 12, 1901, a fine spring evening indeed.

It would take the entire night for all 141 feet of the schooner-barge's hull to amble the 70 odd miles to the mouth of the Saginaw River. This was a trip that the Montmorency had made hundreds of times in all kinds of weather but, in these opening days of the 1901 navigation season, the buoys that mark the way to the river had yet to be placed. No matter, her captain set a course of 220 degrees and pushed for the mouth of the river.

Good fortune seemed to be smiling on the Montmorency tonight as the wind picked up and began to speed her progress. No one onboard had the slightest inkling that the boat was about to become a sidelight in the most tragic storm in Saginaw Bay's history. With her sails filling, the boat gained momentum. The mass of her cargo of 400,000 board feet of lumber now gave her a good bit of forward inertia. All of this just in time for one of the Charity Islands to get in the schooner-barge's way. In the pitch black of the night the barge ran hard onto Little Charity Island. With a shocking jolt the boat stuck fast on the unlighted island. Apparently that brisk spring wind that had quickened the barge's pace had also caused her to stray from the unmarked path she should have been on. Now she would be stuck there until she could be pulled off.

The following day the tug Ella Smith sailed out to pull the barge off. After pulling for most of the day the big tug finally gave up and returned to Bay City reporting that the barge would require lightering in order to be removed from the island. Three days later the tug returned with a lighter and began removing the Montmorency's cargo. At about this same time the steamer Baltimore was steaming from the Port of Lorain, Ohio. She pulled behind her a large flat barge and a small scow. Captain M.H. Place was guiding her through the clutter of vessels working the port. The oak steamer had come from the Linn and Craig shipyard at Gebraltar Michigan in 1881 as the Escanaba, and measuring a respectable 212 feet in length, 35 feet in beam and 20 feet in depth was considered to be one of the giants of her time. In 1899 she was taken over by P.H. Fleming, given the name Baltimore, and quickly blended into obscurity with a hundred others of her class.

As the Baltimore slid past the noisy Lorain waterfront into the quiet of a calm Lake Erie, a single, inconspicuous figure stood propped against the boat's aft rail. Second Engineer Thomas Murphy watched quietly as the details of Lorain began to fade. On deck, George McGinnis was puttering with one of the boat's hatch planks. Aside from the rare occasion when their duties caused the two sailors to cross paths, Murphy and McGinnis rarely associated with one another. The situation was not one of dislike, simply distance. Two different men of different rank doing different jobs. Before this trip to the Soo would come to an end, their paths would cross in a way that neither could now imagine in their wildest nightmares.

Shortly after dinner on Tuesday, May 21, 1901, the Baltimore pushed upbound past Port Huron and onto a rather ugly Lake Huron. Stiff winds and a modest chop met the boat and her tows at the southern end of the big lake. A powerful spring gale was brewing across the Lakes and the wind began to blow strongly from the northeast. Spring gales of this kind are not uncommon along the Lakes, and even if they do not contain the ice cold winds and thick snows of their fall counterparts, their winds can be extremely strong. In fact, 85 years later the modern giants of the lakes would be as vulnerable to the spring storms as their tiny wooden predecessors. A case in point being May 1, 1986, when the Wolverine and William R. Roasch, were both pinned to the dock wall by a spring gale blowing down Saginaw Bay. On the stormy May evening in 1901, Captain Place pushed his boat into Lake Huron with little regard for the weather. After all, the Baltimore with her inspector's rating of A-l, and her belly full of coal should be able to handle a tad of weather with a few groans at worst.

Off Little Charity Island the Ella Smith and her lighter were unable to continue work on the Montmorency in the face of the building northeaster. The tug and her charge made a hasty run for the Saginaw River, and no sooner had she left the scene of the barge's stranding than the crew of the Montmorency went over the side and sought shelter on the uninhabited island. As circumstance would have it, the luckless schooner-barge was fetched up on the northeast side of the island directly in the face of the storm. Reaching Bay City, the master of the Ella Smith hustled to the office of Mr. William H. Sharp, Manager of the barges James L. Ketchum, and Montmorency. Although the boats were owned by the King estate, it was Mr. Sharp who shuffled their ports and cargoes. The report from the tug Smith's master was not good. Wind and waves had forced him to abandon his chore of lightering the barge with over 160,000 feet of lumber still onboard. For the remainder of the day Mr. Sharp could do nothing more than gaze through his office window toward the low gray clouds that hung over the bay, as the wind pulled and beat upon the glass. He alone knew that the Montmorency carried no insurance policy.

Through the night steamer Baltimore fought head to the storm. In the boat's cramped galley Captain Place's wife, who served as stewardess, tried to busy herself. The chore of soaking up floods of lake water and juggling dishes and cups that seemed to leap from the cupboards kept her occupied throughout the frustrating night. Forward in the pilothouse Captain Place kept a close eye on the condition of his boat.

Near the northern end of Lake Huron, First Mate Michael Brethren popped into the pilothouse his clothing soaked with ice cold lake water. He informed the captain that Chief Marooux had found water leaking into the cargo hold, and that the aft washroom had been broken in by the seas. As the captain pondered turning to run before the storm the angry Lake made the decision for him. A giant wave broke green over the Baltimore's bow and charged the length of her spardeck. Slamming into the boat's after deckhouse, the mountain of icewater caved-in the engineer's quarters and sweeping away all of their possessions. Fearing that the Baltimore was about to founder, Captain Place turner the boat abeam of Thunder Bay and began to run southwest with the storm.

Tawas would be the next practical shelter 60 miles to the southwest. The big hook of land that is Tawas Point juts nearly two miles long into Lake Huron and offers perfect shelter from any northern gale. As the Baltimore ran toward the Point her pumps began to lose ground against the intruding lake water. Rolling high on the crest of each wave and the wallowing deep into the valley of water between, it was difficult to see that the boat was slowly sinking deeper into the lake with each passing minute.

At six a.m., off Au Sable Point and 14 miles from the safety of Tawas, the Baltimore rose to the crest of an unusually large wave and then slid down the front side. With bone-jarring jolt the wooden steamer struck heavily on the bottom. Crumpling like a china doll, the Baltimore broke in two just aft of the forward deckhouse. A second giant wave broke over her and carried away the deck accommodations and the lifeboats atop them. Another sea toppled the shattered boat's smokestack. A stunned Crew scrambled on deck. Engineer Murphy was standing stunned near Mrs. Place when her husband charged toward them shouting, "it's every man for himself now." The words seemed to echo through Murphy's shock, as did the look of despair on the face of the captain's wife.

Taking their captain's orders to heart the sailors began to fend for themselves. Some took to the rigging, hoping against hope that the Baltimore wouldn't go to pieces beneath them. Others began to lash themselves to floatable wreckage. Some simply floundered about in blind panic among the flotsam. Engineer Murphy grabbed deckhand McGinnis and directed him to lash himself to a rigbolt attached to a piece of what had been the after cabin. No sooner had the two men secured themselves to the make-shift raft then a giant sea cascaded over the entire scene and swept the wreck clean.

Ashore in Bay City the storm of wind was raising equal havoc as it was on the lake. At the Pitts and Company mill of Bay City, one of their tall smokestacks came crumbling down. On the south end of Bay City, at the Campbell and Brown lumber company, half a million feet of logs that had been tied into a raft were broken loose by the wind. Also at the Hitchcock lumber company a sizable raft was broken loose. Both the floats of logs drifted upstream and fouled against the Cass Avenue bridge. The lumber tug Maud S. was dispatched to re-open the blocked river channel. Meanwhile the 47 foot schooner George Davis crashed ashore at midmorning. Enroute from Au Gres to Bay City the tiny schooner had dropped her anchors off Wenona Beach before dawn. A short time later the chains parted and Captain Fitzgibbon and Mate Smith were forced to raise sail for Bay City. No sooner had they started their run than the boat's rudder chains broke and the helpless little schooner drifted ashore. The angry spring gale was having an open brawl all along Saginaw Bay.

Atop their makeshift liferaft, Murphy and McGinnis saw the late dawn illuminate a dark gray sky. After being washed over the Baltimore's side the two men came to the surface still tied to the piece of wreckage that Murphy had so hastily selected. Floundering low in the water they couldn't see what had become of the Baltimore, in fact they were much too busy simply trying to keep their heads above the water. A short time after they'd been adrift McGinnis began to panic and thrash about insanely. He tried to untie himself twice and both men nearly drowned as Murphy struggled to relash him.

With their bodies numbed by the frigid water the two sailors spent the morning fighting for life within sight of land. Each time McGinnis would begin to get loose, Murphy would calm him by saying that he could see a boat coming, and to just hold on. Finally at mid-morning the 141 foot passenger steamer City of Holland came into view.

Murphy held McGinnis down with one arm and waved with the other. he shouted with every bit of energy remaining in his soul, but the Holland steamed right past. No one onboard ever saw the two ship-wrecked sailors.

Concerned over the well-being of the stranded Montmorency, and unaware of the Baltimore's wreck, the Tawas Lifesavers launched their boat and began to pull for Little Charity Island. When they arrived they found the wooden barge going to pieces but her crew was nowhere to be found. Of course what the lifesavers also didn't know was that the Montmorency's crew were safe and warm around a fairly large bon fire built from their boat's cargo.

During the previous night the tug Columbia had lost her tow of a government dredge and two loaded lighter barges into the storm. Unknown to Murphy and McGinnis, the Columbia's loss would be the event that would spare them from a frozen doom. While criss-crossing the bay in search of its lost tow the Columbia came upon a chunk of a shattered steamer and on it two sailors near death. After dragging the raft's passengers aboard, the tug quickly took sailors Murphy and McGinnis to Tawas where they could begin the long process of recovery. The Columbia then returned to her search for her consorts.

On Friday, May 24, the E.B. Foss's 152 foot steamer Benton pushed into the Saginaw river towing the 163 foot barge G.K. Jackson. The two had run downbound from Georgian Bay heels to the storm. It was the fastest passage they had ever made. On that same day the Montmorency was declared a total loss, and the tug Columbia pulled into the Soo with her wayward dredge and barges in tow. What remained of the Baltimore was found; it was simply her machinery and a few broken hull timbers. The scow and flat-barge that the steamer had in tow were never seen again. Also on this pleasant Friday, Thomas Murphy watched the blue lake from his bed at Tawas, knowing that when every man went for himself, he had managed to save another.

After the **Escanaba** was renamed **Baltimore** in 1899, her trade remained primarily in iron ore. Unfortunately she would only work the blue water trade for a few months under her new name.

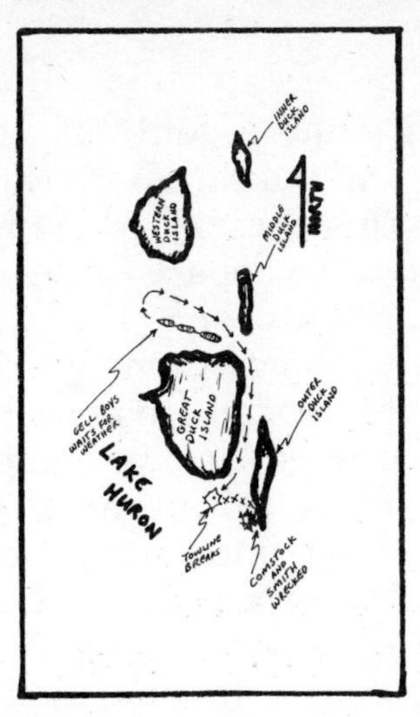

A Shack On Duck Island

Stepping from his cabin, Captain Charles Loynes gave the extra tug necessary to close his slightly warped cabin door. This morning he had awakened at the Port of Collingwood, Ontario, in the southernmost tip of Georgian Bay. Looking across the deck of his command, the schooner-barge Abram Smith, Captain Loynes could see that the majority of the cargo had been loaded. As usual the Smith would be hauling lumber to Bay City, Michigan, 449,000 board feet of it this trip, valued at just over 5,000 dollars. A mixture of 149,000 feet of finely cut "good lumber" was stacked atop 300,000 feet of coarse pine. The whole load was consigned to the Mershon, Schuette, and Parker Company. Captain Loynes could readily see that his cargo was well stacked and ready for sailing.

A low October sky was hanging over this Sunday morning. In fact, Captain Loynes's sailing sense told him that a foul bit of weather was brewing across the Lakes. There was no real worry about weather this Sunday morning, after all the Smith wasn't due to depart Collingwood until the next day, Monday, October 8, 1906. That's when the steamer Langell Boys was scheduled to pick her up. Until then the old wooden schooner-barge could only wait, snugly moored to the now empty lumber dock.

Shortly after midnight the tiny lumber hooker Langell Boys pulled away from the Rustic lumber dock at Bying Inlet, Ontario, on the northeast coast of Georgian Bay. This little steamer was a frequent sight in and along the Saginaw River where she sometimes made as many as two arrivals a week. Steaming southeast along the Ontario coast in the pre-dawn hours of Monday , October 8, the Langell Boys was on the way to Midland, Ontario, to pick up the schooner barge J. B. Comstock which had loaded over 400,000 board feet of lumber at that port. The steamer,which was also loaded with a full cargo of lumber, would then haul for Collingwood to pick up the Abram Smith and pull both barges to Bay City. After a choppy 78 mile push the Langell Boys rounded Pinery and Asylum points and slid into Midland. Less than 20 minutes later the steamer and barge departed for Collingwood to pick up the Smith.

Captain Loynes arose early Monday morning, knowing that around dawn the Langell Boys would come puffing down off the Bay to take his boat in tow. As expected, the dim light of Monday's late dawn illuminated the square outline of the lumber hooker that was inbound to take on the schooner. In the distance was the silhouette of the Comstock; The Langell Boys had to drop the Comstock about a mile out of Collingwood. The encumberment of the barge didn't allow the steamer enough maneuverability to pick up the Smith. By dropping the first barge, the steamer could easily swing in and put a line aboard the Smith. Once out of the confines of Collingwood Harbor, the steamer would pull across the bow of the Comstock, who would then become the last boat in the string.

By the time the three lumber boats began pushing northwest toward Cove Passage and then on to the open surface of Lake Huron, a wicked gale had started to blow. The stiff October wind came roaring across Lake Superior at first. There the steamer Gladstone was downbound from Two Harbors with the barge Pasadena in tow. Both boats were carrying better than full loads of iron ore when the storm grabbed hold of them. In the face of the growing southwester, the Gladstone ran for shelter, the closest of which was Portage Lake in the middle of Michigan's Keweenaw Peninsula. To get there the steamer and her consort would have to enter and navigate down the Portage ship channel. As they entered the channel the Gladstone cleared well, but a sudden burst of wind ripped the Pasadena from the steamer and impaled her on the rocks of the harbor entrance. Giant seas burst over the stricken vessel plucking away her deck gear and most importantly her lifeboat. Beneath the feet of her 10 crewmen the Pasadena began to breakup. The situation had become so desperate so fast that her crew decided the only route to survival was over the side and through the rampaging surf. Out of the 10 crewmembers who leaped into the trashing ice water, three did not survive the swim.

When the Langell Boys and her two barges plowed through Cove Passage, they met a furious Lake Huron. The southwest wind was blowing over

40 miles per hour and 15 foot seas came charging against the three wooden boats. A nightmarish fog formed in the valleys between the cresting waves as the ice cold wind blew across the less cold lake water. Turning on a 225 degree magnetic heading the steamer pointed toward Saginaw Bay.

The south, southeast wind quickly proved to be too much for the over-burdened and under-powered Langell Boys. When fully loaded and pulling two loaded barges the steamer could hardly make seven miles an hour in clam weather, now she was actually being blown backward across the open Lake. By dinner-time Monday, the three lumber carriers had been blown 30 miles north of where they should have been. The only choice now that would keep the three boats from being beaten to the bottom of the Lake was to turn and run for shelter.

As luck would have it, the storm had blown the trio within reach of the five Duck Islands. Just before dark, the three mauled boats dropped their hooks in the lee of Great Duck Island. With the wind and seas now broken, the heavily loaded boats could now rest until the storm subsided.

Onboard the Abram Smith, Captain Loynes did not sleep, instead he stayed awake into the night with an eye to the weather. During the late hours of the night he felt the wind slowly change direction. The Captain knew too well that Great Duck would only afford lee to the three boats until the wind began to blow from the west. Then the vessels would be exposed and could possibly be blown on to the island itself. By daylight the wind had turned beyond west and began blowing from the west, northwest. From the Smith, Captain Loynes saw the surf exploding over Middle Duck Island half a mast high.

Soon the Langell Boys raised the signal to up anchor and the three boats made for the other side of the island. Wheeling to the right, the steamer tugged her consorts around 180 degrees. Threading the half mile gap between Middle and Great Duck Islands, the three boats pushed toward the southern end of Great Duck Island. There was great logic in this move. The wind was continuing to shift and would soon be blowing from a more northern quarter. In this case, the south end of the big island would offer the best protection in the hours to come.

Passing through the narrow channel between outer Duck Island an Great Duck Island, the Langell Boys turned to round the southern end of the big island. The trio was rudely surprised to find that even though the wind was now whipping from the west, northwest, the seas were still rolling heavily from the south. In turning to round the south end of the island, all three boats were now exposed to a quartering head sea, and began to cork-screw. This action proved to more than the thick towing hawser could handle.

Captain Loynes felt sure that the Abram Smith could handle the weather as long as she were kept in lee of one of the islands. When the boats were exposed to the rolling south sea however, the first wave smashed away the Smith's knight head, and a moment later the towline to the Langell Boys parted. Feeling that his boat, and the J.B. Comstock which was tied to the Smith's stern, were now adrift in the gale, Captain Loynes let go the anchors and began paying out the chain. Like two chunks of driftwood, the barges were being blown with the wind directly toward Outer Duck Island, less than a mile astern.

Like the Smith, the Comstock let go her

anchors too. Soon both schooner-barges had let out their chains two the bits. The giant iron hooks simply dragged across the lake bottom. Astern on the Smith's rail. Captain Loynes watched in horror as the south shore of Outer Duck Island loomed before him. With an agonizing crunch and the sound of tortured planking, the Abram Smith slammed onto the rocks. A deafening groan sounded above the storm as the Smith's oak hull twisted out of shape. Moments later a series of waves pounded her firmly onto Outer Duck Island.

As Captain Loynes's crew mustered at the barge's yawl preparing to abandon ship, the J.B. Comstock crashed ashore nearly taking off part of the Smith's starboard side. Once again the groan of planking filled the air as the Comstock settled on her keel and broke in two. Although wedged frighteningly close to the Smith, the Comstock's position was a blessing in disguise. The barge's broken hull blocked the foaming surf, and provided a sheltered escape for the yawls of both boats. All but one sailor, who refused to leave the Smith, made it to dry land safely.

Once on Outer Duck Island, the soaking wet castaways quickly realized that their immediate need was shelter from the October wind. Captain Loynes solved this problem quickly. Calculating that both boats would soon go to pieces, he ordered the sailors to gather as much of the cargo lumber that had washed off the wrecks as they could carry. In the woods near the beach the shipwrecked sailors fashioned a small shack to break the wind. More of the cargo was used to build a large bon fire around which they all huddled throughout the frozen night.

In the morning the familiar lines of the Langell Boys appeared in the mist. Searching for her lost consorts, the steamer chanced upon the wreck sight. The Comstock was a total loss and practically in pieces. The Smith was resting upright on her shattered bottom. Both boats were in about 12 feet of water.

The majority of the two crews were taken onboard the Langell Boys, who with her cargo intact, steamed for Bay City. Several crewmembers as well as the Comstock's master remained behind to watch over what remained of the lumber cargoes. Weeks later, before winter's ice closed the 1906 navigation season, the cargoes from both wrecks were salvaged. The hulks of the once proud lumber vessels were left behind, considered to be total losses.

Today, nothing remains of the lumbering era on the Lakes. The vast fleet of white oak boats are gone and the ports that once served them are over grown by nature or reshaped by modern population. Those remote ports in northern Lake Huron are sparsely populated and in many cases abandoned to become fresh water ghost towns. Anyone visiting Collingwood or Blind River would never guess that they were once a simple lumber port and a bustling boom town, respectively. And if exploring the isolated woods of Outer Duck Island one might easily overlook the scant remains of a tiny makeshift shack that once meant the survival of nearly a dozen shipwrecked sailors on a frozen stormy night in 1906.

Address Unknown

The first hints of spring were just beginning to overshadow winter's last gasps on a blustery Saturday, April 20, 1901. It was then that the steel hull of the steamer Uranus got its first taste of freshwater when she slid down the ways at the Detroit Shipbuilding company's Wyandotte facility. She was launched into a time of frantic growth in the Great Lakes' shipping industry. Lake boats were being turned out at such a steady pace that in a couple of cases, there were no christening ceremony at all. Vessels of Uranus's size splashed sideways into the brackish backwaters around the lakes in a seemingly endless parade. Noteworthy to the Uranus's story was the launching of the 404 foot package freighter Wilkesbarre five months earlier, in December of 1900. In another era, these two vessels would find their end together in a way that no person at their launching would have imagined.

A good working size was the Uranus's most noteworthy attribute. Being far short of the giant 500 footers that were just starting to appear on the lakes, the Uranus's 366 foot length was about average for the ore boats of her day. She would carry a belly full of the red gold that was iron ore from the upper lakes, then return with profitable cargo of coal in her hold. When the Gilchrist company took delivery of her in 1901, she went straight to work doing exactly that.

The Uranus's look was as typical as the job that she performed. Her fo'c'sle was half raised, or only elevated about four feet from her spar deck. Atop the fo'c'sle was planted a very average looking round pilothouse with officers quarters attached to its back. Looking aft a service of 12 hatches covered the boat's shoebox-like cargo hold. At her stern was rectangular deckhouse where her engine and galley crew were quartered. From a distance it was difficult to distinguish her profile from nearly two dozen other ore boats sailing with her exact measurements.

Both the Uranus and the Wilkesbarre became parts of a massive work force of machines and men that labored around the clock hauling ore, coal, stone, grain, and other cargos from the time the first boat could smash her way out of the channel ice in March, until December's winter grip froze the waterways solid again. There was always more work for more boats and more men. The route plodded by the Uranus was usually the same as that of the Wilkesbarre, with the ore boat running from upper Lake Superior's ore docks to Lake Erie's steel mill and the package freighter pushing from the upper lake's growing communities to the lower lakes bustling cities. On nearly a weekly basis the two vessels hooted the standard passing signals at one another. In the first decade of the 1900's, it appeared as if the only limits to Great Lakes shipping were the number of boats that could be produced and the number of men that could be found to man them. Surely nothing could ever stop such prosperity.

Just over 30 years after the Uranus was launched, the world had changed drastically. A global depression had shattered the economic foundation of nearly every civilized nation in the northern hemisphere. In the industrialized countries such a the United States, the effect of the Great Depression were particularly devastating. Millions of able-bodied Americans drifted about the countryside without work, self-respect or even hope. There was no welfare, no unemployment compensation, no food stamps; programs in government aid simply did not exist. Good fortune was not having a job, good fortune was simply having a meal.

Around the Great Lakes, industry was heavily depressed. Countless factories were vacated with their equipment left rusting. what remained of the fleet of wooden lakeboats were abandoned wherever they happened to be moored. Now their hulls were picked apart by destitute people in need of firewood or their deckhouses became the haven for homeless drifters in search of shelter. Most of the steel fleet of ore boats could be found moored haphazardly to nearly any dock where they could be laid up. The only reason for many of the boats not going to scrap was the fact that the scrap market was just as depressed as every other industry. Vessel owners found it more economical to simply leave their boats rusting at the lay-up wall than to scrap them. During most of the 1930's, few lakeboats found gainful hauling, and those that did were manned by sailors whose experience and ratings far outweighed the position in which they were employed. Captains could be found working as mates, mates working as wheelsmen, cooks as porters chiefs as oilers and so on. In those days of the Great Depression, any employment was a godsend.

The fall of 1934 found the Uranus sailing under a new company's flag with a new name. She now sailed for the Algoma Central Railway as the W.C. Franz. She had spent most of the 1934 season waiting idle at the lay-up dock and had been brought out to participate in the fall grain rush, or what there was of a grain rush. Late in the day on November 18, the W.C. Franz finished unloading her cargo of wheat at Port Colborne. Hours later, her hatches tightly sealed, the Franz joined the westbound course across Lake Erie. This was a path that the 33-year old boat had traveled many times before. Her ore carrying days were far behind her now and perhaps that was a good thing. Laid up in each port city that she steamed past were members of the Franz's former brethren of ore boats, some over 600 feet long. Now the Franz's job was simple to go to Fort William, Ontario for another load of Canadian grain. Perhaps when she reached Port Colborne to again unload, word would be waiting that the economic times would not require her to make another run. Her beam would be again put to the lay-up wall and her crew would be laid off for another indefinite period of time. For the moment however, the Franz and her crew were just lucky to have a gainful cargo assignment; if another followed, so much the better.

Most of the next two days were taken up by the Franz's passage across Lake Erie, up the Detroit River, through Lake St. Clair and up the St. Clair River. Tuesday afternoon, November 20, found the W.C. Franz pushing her bluff bow into a dead calm Lake Huron. A layer of warm stable air had settled over the Great Lakes region and a thick foggy haze had developed atop the ice cold lake water. As is typical of this type of late season temperature inversion, not only had the fog developed, but every bit of the black sooty smoke that roller from the Franz's funnel remained trapped low to the water where it lingered long after the boat had passed.

At about the same time as the W.C. Franz was clearing Harbor Beach, another boat was entering northern Lake Huron. Steaming downbound into the glassy water came the Great Lakes Transit Corporation's pack freighter Edward E. Loomis. A close discerning eye could recognize her lines as being the former Wilkesbarre. Much like the Franz, she had changed owners and names. Now she was picking her way through the Depression carrying anything that could be put in her hold. Survival meant performing her chores without causing her owners any undue expense. Tonight, the Loomis was bound out of Milwaukee under the command of Captain Angus McKenzie. At eight o'clock however, Captain McKenzie was relieved of his pilothouse watch by First Mate Joseph LaMontague. The good captain had stood his command nearly all the way from Milwaukee and through the Straits of Mackinaw. Now it was his time for a well earned rest.

Somewhere between the converging Loomis

and Franz, a pint-sized lakeboat was steaming upbound on a pitch black Lake Huron. Hissing quietly upbound was the Paterson Steamship Line's 259 foot canaler, Soreldoc. This six year old steamer was one of a great fleet of tiny steel vessels that were specifically designed to fit the "old" locks of the Welland Canal. In the first decades of the 1900's, these vessels scurried about the Great Lake, over 200 steamers strong. During the dark days of the Depression however, most of these efficient little freshwater tramps ere crowed into any lay-up port the same as their giant ore carrying counterparts. On this November night, the Soreldoc was working her way through the Depression Like the Loomis, carrying anything that could be put in her or on her. A hold full of coal was as common as a deckload of automobiles. There was no way for the crew of the Soreldoc to know that in a few hours, through no fault of their own, the vessel would play an instrumental role in the biggest shipwreck of 1934.

By midnight, a modest breeze had started to wisp across Lake Huron from the south. The direction and speed of this draft was just right to grab the thick black coal-smoke from the Franz's tall smokestack and spread it across her deck and far out ahead of her. It was the kind of wind that the pilothouse crews of the old coal fired steamers loathed. It cut visibility to a confusing sooty charcoal gray. In the days before the Environmental Protection Agency and public concern over pollution, thick blankets of coal smoke were just a fact of life that everyone learned to live with.

Captain Alex McIntyre, master of the W.C. Franz, was sound asleep in his quarters by the time his boat came upon the lights of the Soreldoc. It was just before two o'clock in the morning on November 21, and from the Franz's pilothouse, First Mate James Gibson peered through the open window. He was doing his best to judge the distance to the vessel he was overtaking. Being that the Franz was designed to haul massive quantities of dense iron ore, she greatly overpowered the tiny Soreldoc, which was designed to work rivers and locks slowly and efficiently. Speedwise, the Franz was having no problem gaining on the canaler; the trouble now was seeing the little boat. In fact, the Soreldoc's own funnel smoke was spreading ahead too, which only compounded the problem.

Head on into the sooty haze of the Franz and Soreldoc's confusion closed the Edward E. Loomis. Like his Canadian counterpart on the W.C. Franz, First Mate LaMontague was squinting through the Loomis's open pilothouse window at the vessel light off her steering pole. Obscured by the haze and funnel smoke, the lights appeared not to be moving and it was difficult to tell if it was one vessel or three vessels. Judging the distance through the black veil of coal soot was also impossible. If the lights were from a few small boats or one of the giant 600 footers. If the smoke was obscuring one of the giant ore carriers, Mate LaMontague still had a few miles before he had to worry about passing.

On the other hand, if they were small boats, he was nearly on top of them. Grabbing the Loomis's whistle pull, he gave two long blows indicating that he would be passing on the oncoming vessels starboard side. From behind the blanket of smoke echoed two deep responses. At the same moment that the Loomis prepared to push by the Soreldoc, the Franz's first Mate made his move to overtake the same boat. Swinging the Franz to starboard, he started around the Soreldoc.

One of the peculiarities of huge masses floating on water is that once you've started in a given direction, it's quite difficult to stop. This means that long before the W.C. Franz and Edward E. Loomis saw one another's lights through the smoke and around the Soreldoc, they were destined to collide.

Onboard the Loomis, First Mate LaMontague suddenly saw many more vessel lights than he had expected. Through the soot it appeared for a moment as if several vessels were hidden by the Soreldoc. Suddenly, the optical illusion caused by the funnel smoke ended and LaMontague came to a sudden sharp realization that sent an ice cold chill to his temples. Another boat was cutting across his bow! Instinctively reaching for the whistle pull, he began to sound a series of short rapid blasts, the traditional danger signal. It was a useless gesture now, there was no power in the universe that could keep the two boats from slamming into one another.

Shortly after three o'clock, on the morning of Wednesday, November 21, 1934, Captain McIntyre, the 71 year old master of the W.C. Franz, was awakened by a jolt to the boat that nearly threw him from his bed. Sitting up in the dark of his cabin, Captain McIntyre felt his boat roll to starboard. Then with the thundering groan of tortured steel, the Franz shuddered and quickly listed to port. Before his next heartbeat, Captain McIntyre knew exactly what happened to his vessel.

When Captain McIntyre reached the pilothouse, he found First Mate Gibson standing ashen-faced on the bridge wing. Off the port side a vessel was hovering, her bow crushed deeply. Looking back over the Franz's listing deck, the captain saw a giant gash in her port side, as if a giant sea monster had bitten into the Franz. It was at this moment that the 71 year old captain's position as the most experienced master on the Great Lakes paid off. At a glance, Captain McIntyre saw that the gash was in the worst possible place. The Franz's hull had been ruptured right at the collision bulkhead. This steel wall that was designed to separate the boat's bow from her cavernous cargo-hold in the event of a head-on collision was now a crumpled vent past which a frigid Lake Huron was now cascading. Without hesitation, Captain McIntyre turned to his first mate and gave the order every master hopes he'll never have to give...

"Lower the boat, Jim," he ordered calmly. His lifetime of experience told him without an inkling of doubt that the Franz was doomed and that action to save his crew had to be taken immediately.

The Franz's bow began to settle quickly as the Abandon Ship signal sounded from her whistle. At this same moment ashore at Alpena, Marine Radio Operator 0. K. Falor was sipping coffee near his trusty wireless set. Suddenly the radio came to life with a frantic stream of Morse Code. The familiar taps of SOS were repeated over and over. Then the chilling message: The steamer Franz had been rammed by another vessel. Falor scribbled the broken message onto his notepad with all the speed and accuracy he could muster. Unfortunately, haste of the sender garbled the most important part of the message, the location. "...halfway between Bay and Thunder Bay..." was all that Falor received. There followed a long moment of graveyard silence that seemed to last for an hour. For a time, Operator Falor feared the sender may have already plunged to Lake Huron's icy depths, then suddenly the wireless came to life again. "Taking to boats now," was all that came over the radio. For a time, the shocked radio operator gazed at his notepad. He knew that at least one, and possibly two lakeboats and their crews were sinking out in the darkness of the big lake and there was little he could do.

Taking a heavy list to port, the Franz had begun to sink hard by the bow. So alarming was the rate of sinking that the boat's radio operator, A. D. Reeser, had only time enough to tap out that brief message. As Reeser dashed to the Franz's deck, he saw Lake Huron coming up at him.

At the freighter's stern, the lifeboats were already being lowered with the port boat coming down first. In this bout were four ill-fated crewmen: Watchman Joseph Langridge, Deckhand Frank Grashville, Steward Hugh Woodbeck and Second Cook Norman Matthews. There was a great deal of haste in lowering the boat and it was well justified. Not only was the Franz looking as if she would go down fast, but the Loomis was beginning to drift up against the Franz's beam. If the lifeboat didn't get away quickly, it could be crushed between the two freighters. Then, without warning, the lowering tackle fouled causing the opposite end of the boat to drop suddenly. All four men in the boat were tossed unceremoniously into Lake Huron's frigid grip. Only Norman Matthews managed to overcome the shock of the ice water and struggle to the surface. An instant later, the heavy wooden lifeboat came crashing down on top of the luckless second cook. Then like a giant vice, the unyielding steel hull of the Loomis squeezed tightly against that of the Franz, crushing the lifeboat like an eggshell.

Now the Franz began to list radically to her

wounded port side. So severe was the list that the starboard lifeboat, which had been lowering, ended up high and dry on the Franz's hull. This left Captain McIntyre and more than a dozen of his crew stranded there waiting for the Franz to sink beneath them, knowing all the while that the suction of the sinking hull would pull them under, too.

As if someone had plugged the giant gash in her side, the W.C. Franz suddenly stopped sinking. Every man involved readily saw this as an opportunity to save the lives of the freighter's crew. A system of three ladders was rigged from the deck of the Loomis to the deck of the Franz. One by one the doomed vessel's crew scurried to the safety of the Loomis. It was a time-consuming process that could have only been accomplished in the glassy sea conditions that happened to exist at the time. Even those stranded in the starboard boat were plucked from their perch. Nearly 45 minutes elapsed from the time the first ladder was placed until the last man crossed to the Loomis. The boat floated, waiting for the sailors to escape, as if the W.C. Franz had been unwilling to take any of her crew with her. Then, quietly the bow began to quickly go under. Her stern, illuminated by the spotlights from the Loomis and Soreldoc, rose high into the night air as the 366 foot vessel slipped to the bottom.

Drifting in silence, the Edward E. Loomis stood by as if in shock. Captain McKenzie knew too well that his boat was far from safe. Her forepeak was stove in nearly through the windlass and she was taking a great deal of water. To compound the problem, the only wireless set on the scene had just plunged to the bottom with the Franz.

Marine Operator Falor had reported the

distress message on his notepad to the Coast Guard, but on the end of his report he had to attach that the location of the collision was unknown. Between Falor and the Coast Guard, every upbound and downbound vessel with a radio was told to be on the lookout for the steamer Franz or her wreckage.

Shortly after five o'clock a.m., the steamer Reiss Brothers, sailing upbound, came upon the tangled lights of the witnesses to the Franz's death. When the Reiss reached the scene, she found the Loomis in a listing condition but apparently not in danger of sinking. The Soreldoc stood nearby waiting in case the Loomis's condition took a turn for the worse. The Reiss Brothers's wireless operator began the busiest watch of his career. He sent the long awaited "next message" from the wreck scene and for the remainder of the day, the Reiss would become the primary source of information concerning the wreck.

At 20 minutes after eight o'clock, on the morning of November 21, the Edward E. Loomis resumed her downbound trip escorted by the Reiss Brothers. With her bow crumpled in and her forepeak filled with water, the Loomis was forced to proceed at half speed.

Some 19 hours after the collision, the Loomis docked at Port Huron. She was met there by a hoard of newspaper men. This army of heavy wool-jacketed vultures descended upon the battered boat with flashbulbs popping and notepads at the ready. About the only story that wouldn't come out of their clamor would be the final epitaph of the Loomis herself. The damages done by the collision, although far from mortal, would be too expensive to repair in these days of the Great Depression. She would spend the next six years rusting in lay-up until the scrap steel demands of World War II justified cutting her up.

As was their job, the reporters quickly gathered as much information about the boats and men as was available. A complete list of the men involved and their home addresses was sent over the wire services. Of those who perished, only Ship's Steward Hugh Woodbeck's hometown was known. Joe Langridge, Frank Grashville and Norm Matthews were all able-bodied nomads that the Depression had forced into a quest for an honest day's work which lead them to sign aboard the Franz. Next to each of their names was simply printed, "Address unknown." This same label can also be attached to the final resting place of the W.C. Franz whose exact location was lost in the confusion on that dark November night. She sits now still headed upbound on Lake Huron's sandy bottom, address unknown.

Absent from the White Oak Graveyard

In an era when most boatyards around the Great Lakes were switching from wooden ship constructions to steel hulls, one man stood stead fast against the current. That man was vessel owner, builder, master, designer and all around wizard James Davidson of Bay City. For nearly 30 years Mr. Davidson operated the most handsome fleet of white oak oreboats on the lakes.

"Ships should be made of wood rather than steel plate...," Davidson would often argue. His reasoning was well thought out and straight forward, too. In the late 1890's and early 1900's, lakeboats were operating in unimproved waterways and shallow upper lake ports with rocky bottoms. When a wooden hull touches a rough bottom or pier, it will give and spring where a steel plate hull will rupture and dent.

On the West Bay City shore of the Saginaw River, Davidson's boatyard spawned more than a dozen giant wooden lakeboats. Steamers and barges in excess of 300 feet in length slid sideways into the murky log-clogged Saginaw River through the late 1890's. These boats quickly entered the long haul ore and coal trade, returning to their birthplace each winter to hibernate until spring. For almost 30 years, this went on until the black years of the Great Depression forced what remained of the Davidson fleet to lay-up for the last time at the abandoned Davidson yard, there to die and rot.

Tall-masted schooner barges of more than 300 feet length that would never see sail were a Davidson trademark. Single word names such as Matanzas, Pretoria, Granada, Abyssinia, Chieftain, Athens, Chickamauga, Algeria, Santiago, Chattanooga and Montezuma meant little to turn of the century boat watcher other than another of Mr Davidson's giant barges was passing. Many times these white oak monsters were being towed by one of the large Davidson steamers. Sacramento, Orinoco, Shenandoah, Panama, Cartagena and Rappahannock were the names given to some of these powerful ore steamers. Across the lakes, James Davidson's fleet was unique and well-known to boat watchers and vesselmen alike.

A steamy Sunday morning, the 23rd of July, 1911, found the Davidson steamer Rappahannock hissing her way clear of the St. Clair River and onto the expanse of Lake Huron. Attached to the steamer's stern by a quarter mile of towing hawser was the Davidson company's 350 foot barge Montezuma. Both boats were out of Ashtabula, Ohio with coal bound for Duluth, Minn. A billow of dense black coal smoke vomited from the

Rappahannock's tall funnel as Captain W.A. Rattray of Marine City ordered full ahead. The lake was flat calm and the black cloud of smoke simply hung near the surface with no breeze to break it up. A heat wave spreading from Iowa to the East Coast had made the last week uncomfortable to say the least. Everywhere around the lakes the air was sticky and stagnated. Onboard the Rappahannock, every door and window was propped wide open, hoping for any hint of a breeze. Below in her cabins, the conditions were smothering. The boat's superstructure tended to retain the heat, and air conditioners or even electric fans were inventions of the future. The weather forecast showed no relief calling for "fair conditions...," a generalized wording so often used in the era before meteorology became a science. By late afternoon, both boats were only silhouettes in the dense summer haze.

At the same time as the two Davidson boats were pushing up Lake Huron, the annual Chicago to Mackinaw Yacht Race was attempting to make progress on Lake Michigan. Only a few wisps of breeze were to be found and all 11 of the most sleek racking yachts on the Great Lakes were making little headway. For the most part, they just sat in the middle of upper Lake Michigan with their sails hanging limply.

On Lake Superior, Michigan's Governor Osborn was the honored guest of the Copper County Naval Reserve onboard the steamer USS Yantic. The part-time sailors who manned the Yantic had put on their best uniforms and polished their vessel to a gleaming excellence to give the state's chief executive the best impression. His was to be a cruise of the greatest comfort and pride.

Unknown to any of those on the Great Lakes

this Sunday, an incredibly strong area of low pressure was pushing across the Canadian border near the Great Plains and was continuing to intensify. Normally, such a low would track with a cold front and spawn a series of thunderstorms 250-350 miles ahead of it. This low however, began to circulate the surrounding atmosphere cyclonically and as it approached the Great Lakes, the storm was big enough to swallow Lakes Huron, Superior and Michigan all at once.

At midmorning on Tuesday, July 25, the Rappahannock and Montezuma locked through the Soo. Mr. Davidson's boats were all good looking and the Rappahannock was no exception. Her 320 foot oak hull sported a curving sheer and her square pilothouse, although typical of a wooden lakeboat, stood like an elegant figurehead atop her raise fo'c'sle. Just over halfway along her spardeck sat a small white deckhouse. Immediately forward of her aft deckhouses was a separate steel boilerhouse from which her tall funnel extended. This separate steel boilerhouse was another of those well thought-out trademarks of Davidson's wooden steamers. It greatly reduced the risk of fire from the boat's own steamworks. When launched in June of 1895, the Rappahannock sported three tall masts with a handsome rake. Now in 1911, the masts were only two, but the boat kept her fine lines in every other way as she entered Lake Superior.

As the unsuspecting pair of Davidson boats hauled into open Lake Superior, a violent cyclone of wind and sheets of rain blasted onto Lake Michigan. There was no warning as the hazy western sky turned dark gray then black-green. Winds quickly grew from nothing to 60 miles per hour with gusts in excess of 75 miles per hour. All of this driving rain from the west-southwest with such fury that the flock of racing yachts that had been pouting on the open laker were scattered and nearly blown over, each losing sight of the other. Two other Davidson boats, the 315 foot steamer Amazonas and her consort the 220 foot Paisley, both on their way to Milwaukee, suddenly found themselves in 20 foot waves and hurricane force winds that would rival any November gale. By nightfall, both boats were losing ground against the storm and being swept toward the Michigan shore.

Clear of Whitefish Point, the Rappahannock and her consort were suddenly struck by a southeast wind and a surprisingly big sea. Captain Rattray decided quickly to turn and meet the wind head-on as it began to shift to east-northeast. Rain smacked on the pilothouse windows making an oscillating "hiss" sound, and it was difficult to see the boat ' s steering pole. Giant green seas soon began to board both boat s and the Rappahannock's oak hull began to groan loudly. After several hours in the wind, waves, and drowning rain, a crewman struggle from the aft cabins toward the pilothouse. He brought forward word that there was a lot of water working around the below decks aft. The Rappahannock had sprung a leak in her oak hull and no one aft was quite sure where it was. Captain Rattray ordered the pumps started, but in less than a half hour, the steamer's sluggish response to the seas told him that the Rappahannock was sinking.

Saving the steamer was now Captain Rattray ' s prime responsibility. Their only chance was to cut loose the Montezuma. Once without her burden, the Rappahannock would have enough power to run for the north shore and the shelter of Jackfish Point.

Cutting a barge loose to find its own end in a storm has always been an accepted practice on the lakes. Most consorts, armed with auxiliary sails and their own anchors, are quite able to survive alone. In fact there are cases where barges cut loose survived and the towing steamer has not. Sometimes however, a barge is cut loose only to drift off into oblivion. With the stroke of an axe, the Montezuma was set free. The Rappahannock's crew watched as the barge blew sideways into the trough of the seas. Rolling heavily, the barge's lamps soon vanished into the sheets of rain and the Rappahannock was alone.

The situation for the Rappahannock was quickly becoming a race for life. Both her steam and hand pumps had been overcome by the incoming water. The leak, wherever it was in her stern, must be massive. Settling lower and lower aft, the boat's spar deck was now constantly swallowed in the swirling water that came breaking over her bow. In her after cabins, the big wooden doors were burst in allowing the wild waters to slosh into her cabins and make flotsam of their contents. One by one the window shutters were being plucked away and several of her windows were smashed. those of her crew not on duty were desperately attempting to rescue their best possessions from the intruding water. Now, Captain Rattray came to the grim conclusion that he only way to save the lives of his crew would be to beach his boat on Jackfish Point. He knew that soon the gaining lake would put out the boat's fires and she would be helplessly blown out onto the open lake in a sinking condition.

Jackfish Point could not be seen from the Rappahannock's pilothouse and Captain Rattray had only his compass and instincts to guide him through the storm, but that was enough. With a bone-jarring shudder and the deafening groan of tortured timbers, the *Rappahannock* ran soundly onto the point shortly before midnight. With an earsplitting hiss and a blinding cloud the boat's engineer let go what steam she had and moments later the in-rushing water put out her fires. Hopefully now there would be no explosion as Lake Superior overtook her boilers.

Immediately the boat's crew took to her lifeboats, led by Captain Rattray. It was a nightmare-like setting; steam poured from every passage and was swept over the departing sailors by hurricane-force winds. Rain pelted them with such violence that it was difficult to open one's eyes and a chore to talk. Men waded waist deep across the spar deck as the lake continued to swallow the steamer. With her bow firmly on the ground, the boat's stern still extended more than 300 feet out into the water where the depth was in excess of 40 feet. As her crew abandoned her, the *Rappahannock* continued to settle below the water. By the time the last yawl was manned, waves were smashing over the deckhouse roof. The entire area became a jumbled mess of floating ropes, casks, pike poles and crates. With desperate rowing, the shipwrecked sailors cleared the boat and made dry land. Captain Rattray, his crew now safe, made for the nearest civilization. His thoughts were now of the drifting *Montezuma*. A communique had to be sent to the Soo so that help could be dispatched to rescue the wayward barge, if she were still afloat.

Before daylight, the telegraph office at the Soo received word of the *Rappahannock*'s wreck along with an urgent plea for aid to the missing

Montezuma. As luck would have it, the Rappahannock's twin sister Sacramento was tied up just above the locks waiting out the storm. No time was wasted in casting off her lines and even as Mr. Davidson was being awakened at his Bay City home with the news of his boats' problems, the Sacramento was pounding out into Lake Superior's rage in search of the Montezuma.

Dawn saw the end of the worst summer storm in Great Lakes history and the light revealed mute evidence of the gale's power. At Buffalo, two of the United States Transportation Company's boats dragged their anchors and were blown ashore. By morning the Harry Colby and W.S. Wilkenson were being pounded on the beach at the foot of Michigan Street. Lake Michigan seemed to be the worst mauled. At South Haven, green apples and peaches were blown from their trees and sucked skyward like bits of paper. The lighthouse at Petoskey was swamped by the sea and its light extinguished. Steaming into the port of Holland four hours overdue was the Graham and Morton steamer Holland. She had been tossed so heavily that her passengers were catapulted from their berths. The Chicago to Mackinaw yachts had been savagely beaten by the gale. Only five had made Mackinaw Island, the first being the Mavourneen. She then dropped anchor, but it failed to hold against the storm and the victorious yacht was smashing on the beach. The yacht Vencidor crashed ashore three miles south of Charlevoix and another yacht crashed onto Beaver island. three others had found shelter along the Michigan Shore. The yacht Illinois however, was not accounted for, and those on Mackinaw Island could gaze out onto the thrashing lake in hope of spotting their missing comrade.

At Glen Arbor, near Grand Traverse Bay, both the Amazonas and Paisley had been blown ashore. As good fortune would have it the lake bottom in that area was sand and neither boat had been heavily damaged. Word was promptly forwarded to Captain Davidson who personally boarded the tug Howard and set out to release his stranded boats.

Steaming into the Soo came the tug Martin with her battered 170 foot consort, the schooner Hattie Wells. The storm had caught them by surprise off of Salt Point and by the time they reached the protection of the St. Mary's River, the schooner's rails had been wrecked, her deck cargo of cedar posts were pillaged and her stern had been stove in. Nearby on Whitefish Bay, 18 other vessels had been in shelter.

Out in the angry surface of Lake Superior the Sacramento was rolling wildly. From near Jackfish Point she would search with the wind in hope of finding the drifting barge or her wreckage. The entire cold stormy day passed as the big steamer retraced the barges drift. Then at sunset, just off Grand Island on Lake Superior's south shore, the Sacramento spotted the familiar outline of the Montezuma. Mr. Davidson's oak giant had been blown more than halfway across Lake Superior and had come within two miles of being dashed on the rocky Michigan shore before the winds suddenly died allowing her anchors to take hold. Quickly a line was put aboard the barge and the Sacramento proceeded to Duluth with the charge that her twin, Rappahannock, had been forced to surrender.

There were a few other happy endings around the lakes after the storm. The battered reserve steamer Yantic made port safely with a shaken

Governor Osborn and a boatload of very seasick weekend sailors. The Amazonas and Paisley were re-floated with help from the tug Howard and the steamer Venezuela on Thursday. So undamaged was the Paisley that the Venezuela towed her on to her original destination. The Amazonas however, had sprung some seams and would have to be taken to Bay City for dry docking. Even the missing yacht Illinois returned from the grave sailing into Mackinaw Island's small harbor sporting battered canvas and a modest list. Only the luckless Rappahannock would sail no more. Her bow now rested firmly in 18 feet of water and her stern was in 45 feet with Lake Superior now smashing her remains.

Today all of Davidson's white oak giants are gone. If however, you happen to be driving north on I-75 near Bay City, Michigan take the U5-10, I-75 Business Loop into the city. In a few miles you will come upon the Veteran's Bridge, and there at the southwest foot of the bridge a small park with low rolling hills. In the park is a giant oak rudder and a short deck that looks out onto the river. Looking closely the remains of the Davidson steamer Shenandoah and the schooner barges Grampian, Granada, Matanzas and Gerritt Smith can be seen just below the river's surface. A plaque mounted on the deck rail maps their resting places. Looking closer at this plaque you'll find that you are standing directly over top of the Montezuma, and that the giant oak rudder over your left shoulder belongs to her rescue steamer Sacramento. The park was once Mr. Davidson's white oak boatyard; it's now a white oak graveyard.

Otto Lindquist's Rude Awakening

Throughout the history of Great Lakes shipping, creative and innovative vessel construction has produced some unique classes of boats. Speculation at the introduction of each of these classes of lakeboats often hailed them as being "the next generation" of laker. So it was with the cigar-shaped whaleback, the Andaste and Choctaw class "monitors" and the giant 300-foot white oak ore barges of the late 1800s. All of these boats were to be the next state of the art in Great Lakes vessels, soon to push all others aside. Even in modern times, the 1000-foot tug/barge combination, and perhaps even the cement carrier barge, may be the next oddball classes that should have been state of the art. None of these classes really became commonplace.

The truly durable classes of lakeboats do not suddenly splash onto the scene with fanfares of things to come. Instead they evolve quietly over time, often in spite of the scoffing of boat buffs and old sailors alike. Today the modern 630-to 730-foot self-unloaders, with all accommodations aft, have quietly taken over the lion's share of the bulk cargo trade. The diversity of the cargoes that these boats can carry, and their efficiency in doing so, created a demand for more of their kind.

Looking back through history, the story has always been the same. With the opening of the modern St. Lawrence seaway came the 730-foot straight-decker, also referred to as "maximum size." Such vessels were the largest size that could transit the seaway. As a result, many of these boats appeared during the decade that followed the opening of the new seaway. Up to that time the largest size vessel that could transit the seaway was 261 feet. Like their successors, these tiny canallers soon became commonplace everywhere around the lakes.

Another unique type of lakeboat came from the drawing board of an innovative marine engineer named Leatham D. Smith. A system by which a boat could unload its cargo at any dockside without the aid of shoreside unloading equipment was his legacy. The first boat fitted with this strange looking array of A-frames, belts and booms was the Hennepen, converted in 1902. She was followed by a vessel specifically designed to accommodate this new contraption. In 1907, the steam Wyandotte was launched as the first vessel constructed totally as a self-unloader. In the early years, as self-unloaders began to appear in greater numbers on the lakes, vesselmen scoffed at their cumbersome deckload of equipment. Surely the A-frame and boom jutting up from an otherwise clear deck would be a ripe target for November's wind and wave. And that boom, what if it should break loose in a storm and swing out over the side? That would finish a boat quickly indeed. Then came the loss of the Clifton and the Andaste, both of whom had recently been converted to Mr. Smith's self-unloader profile. This only fueled speculation that such equipment was unseaworthy. In modern times, however, it is rare to see a lakeboat running that is not a self-unloader.

When she slid down the builder's ways in May of 1890, the lakeboat S.R. Kirby was the largest example of one of the most unique concepts in lakeboat construction. Iron-hulled to the point where her sides began to round under, the Kirby's bottom was of white oak planking. This type of hull construction was called "composite," referring to the fact that these boats were a sort of link between the old wooden hulls and the steel giants of the future. At 311 feet overall, the Kirby was the largest composite vessel ever constructed.

There are varying schools of thought as to why composite hulls came into being. Some say that there was an underlying mistrust of steel and iron hulls among the vesselmen. The result was that a hull made of inexpensive steel, whose bottom was sheathed in a more expensive white oak, would draw more confidence from vesselmen and insurance underwriters, and thus a lower insurance rate than a pure metal hull. Another theory is that since boats serving the rocky ports of the upper lakes often came in contact with jagged boulders lurking beneath the water, a wooden bottom was much better able to spring to an occasional impact than would be a steel or iron bottom. Whatever the reason, the S.R. Kirby went to work one month after her launching for the Northwestern Transportation Company.

The Kirby's profile was a bit more boxy than the average laker. Her Texas cabins and pilothouse accommodation were set back from her fo'c'sle and stacked directly on her spardeck just aft of her number one hatch. Evenly spaced along the spardeck behind the Texas were two "doghouse"-style deck cabins. To top things off, the Kirby started her life sporting three tall rakish masts. Below, in her engine room, the Kirby's builders at the Detroit Dry Dock Company had constructed a powerful triple expansion steam engine. In those early years of the 1890s the S.R. Kirby was indeed the queen of her class.

On the crisp spring morning of Sunday, May 7, 1916, church bells echoed against the giant wood pilings of the Ashland, Wisconsin ore dock. Poised below squatted the S.R. Kirby and her steel consort, the George E. Hartnell. The wafting aroma of sizzling bacon snaked its way around the loading dock. Emanating from the Kirby's galley, the smell scented the still morning air. As Captain Dave Girardin strolled aft toward breakfast, the only interruption of the morning's quiet was the rumble of iron ore down the chutes. There was no day of rest on this Sunday. After all, across the Atlantic ocean the first World War was raging. The free world was hungry for wartime steel, and the primary source of the ore used to make that steel was the Upper Great Lakes. As long as there was a war, there would be plenty of work for the ore boats.

A calm Lake Superior greeted the Kirby as she steamed from Ashland Harbor with the Hartnell in tow. In this, her 26th season of toil, the Kirby sported a slightly different silhouette than she had when her career began. Gone was the middle of her three spars and also missing was the aftermost of her two doghouses. Her open-air flying bridge now was enclosed with a box-like pilothouse. Even with these changes, the Kirby still carried the elegant look that was constructed into her generation of lakeboat.

Down in the Kirby's firehold, Stoker Otto Lindquist was sweating at the backbreaking toil of feeding the steamer's boilers. A stoker's job in the era of hand-fired boilers was hellish. The firehold was a dark dingy passageway often lit only by a couple of dim incandescent light bulbs. Temperatures normally hovered near the hundred-degree mark. Those who worked the firehold were always covered with sweat and coal dust. Because of this, the men who fired the boilers of lakeboats were commonly known as "the black gang." Rarely were these crewmen aware of the doings of their boat; they simply labored in their private purgatory, emerging only for sleep and meals. So, when the Kirby's firedeck began to pitch under Lindquist's feet, he knew that the boat was coming into some weather. He just didn't know how much weather.

A sudden spring gale had sprung up around the Kirby and her consort, and was rapidly building to frightening strength. Such storms rival the fury of their November counterparts and are the loathsome enemy of the lakeboats and their crews. Although they are normally of shorter duration than fall storms, the spring gales seem to explode without warning and enrage the lakes into a greater violence. This particular spring blow had started from the northwest and was soon spitting wind gusts of over 60 miles per hour.

Lindquist had finished his early morning watch at 8:00 a.m. and without regard to the nasty weather, the exhausted stoker retired to his bunk. At about this same time the 524-foot steamer E.H. Utley, followed closely by the 569-footer Joseph H. Block, came into sight of the Kirby and Hartnell. On board the Utley, Captain C.C. Balfour was in charge of over 10,300 tons of iron ore bound from Duluth down to South Chicago. To him the Kirby and her barge were now just a smudge of coal smoke on the stormy horizon, but in the next three hours, Captain Balfour and his crew would get a horrifyingly close look at the S.R. Kirby that would make them regret ever seeing her at all.

As the Utley drew close to rounding the Keweenaw Peninsula, the boat was taking giant seas at her port stern quarter. The waves, some in excess of 50 feet, were violently corkscrewing the Utley. Her stern was being pushed high into the air and her deck twisted like a serpent with each wave that ran along her. It was with this twisting, or "working," in mind that the Utley's master looked with concern, that when his vessel was about to overtake the Kirby he signalled, by whistle, to see if the boat was in need of any kind of assistance. There was no reply from the steamer or her barge. Somehow that just wasn't good enough for Captain Balfour, who ordered all available hands to keep an eye on the slower Kirby which was slowly being left behind by the Utley. This he noted in the boat's log; the time was 10:00 a.m.

At 40 minutes after 10:00, Otto Lindquist was rudely awakened when a jolt to the Kirby tossed him from his bunk, dumping him without dignity onto the floor. It took a minute or so for the confused stoker to regain his senses. Then he quickly realized his boat was in a bad way. Dashing to the deck, clad only in his underwear, Lindquist first felt the biting cold wind pulling at his hair. Huge hills of ice water rising higher than the Kirby's stack surrounded the steamer. He stood there silently in awe of Superior's clutches for nearly five minutes.

Then a sound like a grinding thunder boom overpowered the roar of the gale-force wind. Lindquist's attention was yanked forward in the direction of the crashing. To his shock, the stoker saw the top of the Kirby's fo'c'sle, as if looking down from her mast. He watched paralyzed as the Kirby's entire bow rose and twisted on the back of a 50-foot wave. The wave appeared to march right at him. Then the boat lurched and the lake burst over the pilothouse, down the hatches, smashed the doghouse and slammed directly into his face like a black block of ice.

Those watching from the E.H. Utley saw the S.R. Kirby swept astern by a giant sea. She teetered on the crest for a moment and then was swept astern by a second sea. With a wave crest at each end and no support between, the boat snapped at the number one hatch just forward of her pilothouse. The Kirby then plunged directly to the bottom of Lake Superior. The crew of the Utley stood on the heaving deck of their boat in shock. No sailor could imagine that any oreboat and her 22 crewmen could be swallowed so quickly, but it had happened right before their eyes. Captain Balfour ordered his boat turned. The E.H. Utley would pound back and attempt to reach the scene in case there were any survivors. It was a risky venture that may cost him his boat, but Captain Balfour knew that if one person had survived and was now thrashing about in the icy lake, it was worth the risk.

Water shot up his nose as Otto Lindquist clawed and kicked at the frigid blackness in which he was immersed. There was no up, no down, no light, no air, only a numbing coldness that shocked every inch of his body. Then suddenly he broke the surface, choking and gasping. Water slapped over his head as he was lifted by a giant wave ,and it was nearly impossible to catch a breath through the spume. Finally able to clear his eyes, Lindquist spotted a large piece of wreckage floating nearby. Stroking for all he was worth, the stoker managed to reach the deckhouse roof and drag himself onto it. Dazed and shivering uncontrollably, he could barely hold onto the big chunk of wreckage. All around him, pieces of flotsam that had once been the S.R. Kirby were being savagely tossed by the towering hills of water. Then through the mess, he spotted Captain Girardin trying to swim toward him. The captain must have been in the pilothouse when the Kirby took her dive and Lake Superior blasted the structure to bits. Lindquist could see that the captain's face was bleeding, as the shipwrecked master of vessels gave a long wave with both arms and then joined his boat in a watery grave. Paddling behind him was his dog and ship's mascot, Tige. Shortly after Captain Girardin passed, his faithful companion followed.

Turning the ore laden E.H. Utley in the 40-to

50-foot seas and a 60-mile-per-hour wind was just short of a miracle. At first the steamer refused to come around and became windlocked in the trough of the seas. Rolling severely, the boat was in a bad place, but Captain Balfour ordered rudder amidship and gained some way in the trough, then hard over and the Utley stuck her nose into the first big wave. Even though the Kirby had been slightly more than a mile behind the Utley, it took more than an hour for Captain Balfour's boat to fight her way back to the wreck site.

The area where the Kirby foundered was a sickening sight. The mile-a-minute wind had already spread the wreckage over a wide area, and the chewing seas had mixed what remained on the surface into a jumbled waste. Otto Lindquist sat tossing on the deckhouse roof, wishing to awaken from this cold nightmare. He closed his eyes, but there was no awakening, his blue lips, chattering teeth and numb fingers were reality. Then, as if to add to his plight, the cabin roof that was keeping him from drowning began to sink. Quickly he began to gather flotsam and fashioned a makeshift raft. There was no way to tell how long it would keep him afloat, but at least he'd have a chance to live, unlike his shipmates who were trapped within the S.R. Kirby on the bottom of Lake Superior.

Through the horror came the E.H. Utley and Joseph Block, belching black smoke and hissing steam. To Otto Lindquist, they were steel saviors. Every member of the boats' crews who weren't passing coal or holding the wheel was on the decks looking for survivors. Nearly a dozen fingers pointed at the bobbin stoker. The Block drew near and a line was tossed. Lindquist wrapped the rope time and time again around his arm and then he clung to it as he had clung to his own life. Hand over hand, his fellow sailors dragged him from Lake Superior's frigid grip.

Now the big lake was setting its sights on another victim. This time it was the Kirby's helpless consort, the steel Hartnell. When the steamer went under, the towline to the barge had parted cleanly. Now the storm had blown the Hartnell around Keweenaw Point and into the bay. The boat had come within a hair of fetching up on Manitou Island. Luckily, the water on the lakeward side of the island is extremely deep and the boat had floated close by without encountering the rocky bottom. Without power or sail, she was now rolling on her beam-ends in the sea trough.

It quickly became apparent to Captain Balfour that there was little chance of recovering any other survivors among the Kirby's wreckage. There were, however, 10 men on the barge Hartnell. Carefully guiding the Utley from the wreckage field, Captain Balfour pressed toward the helpless barge.

The good captain's assumption regarding other survivors was wrong. Shortly after the Utley departed, the steamer Harry Berwind, upbound to Duluth, appeared on the scene to pluck Joseph B. Burda from the wreckage. Burda, the Kirby's second mate, had been clinging to some floating wreckage and was nearly unconscious when the Berwind pulled near and rescued him.

Nearly three hours after the steamer S.R. Kirby was bitten in half by Lake Superior, her consort the Hartnell was recovered. The E.H. Utley, with the orphaned barge in tow, proceeded to the Soo to tell the story. Leading the Utley to the Soo was the Joseph Block with her additional shivering passenger, Otto Lindquist. Cradling a hot cup of coffee in his hands, Lindquist watched as a continuously angry Lake Superior flung itself against the Block's galley portholes. Between the green waves, glimpses of the E.H. Utley and the Hartnell could be seen all the way en route to the Soo. Behind the oreboats remained the S.R. Kirby's wreckage field churned by an ill-tempered but ever-patient Lake Superior. Now Superior would wait for the next oreboat that would be her victim, and for the next Otto Lindquist who would witness her terror and live to tell about it.

Bibliography

Fresh Water Whales	Wright
Munising Shipwrecks	Stonehouse
Seaway Review (Autumn 1980)	Lesstrang Publishing Co.
Lake Carriers	Lesstrang Publishing Co.
Went Missing	Stonehouse
Great Lakes Ships We Remember (Vol. I & II)	Van Der Linder
A Pictorial History of the Great Lakes	Hatcher & Walter
Shipwrecks of the Lakes	Bowen
Ghost Ships of the Great Lakes	Boyer
True Tales of the Great Lakes	Boyer
Namesakes (1900-1909, 1910-1919, 1920-1929)	Greenwood
The New Namesakes of the Lakes	Greenwood
Namesakes II	Greenwood
Great Lakes Shipwrecks and Survivals	Ratigan
The Telescope (Vol. XXV-XXXVI)	Great Lakes Maritime Institute
Bay City Times (and Tribune) (4/24/1886 - 12/14/1963)	

Letters and additional information from Mr. D. Ward Fuller, C.E.0., American Steamship Company and Captain John Allen, American Steamship Company, 1987.

While searching for her wayward tow the tug **Columbia** stumbled upon the remains of the **Baltimore** and second engineer Thomas Murphy.

Courtesy of Milwaukee Public Library

Seen here at a Cleveland dock in the Fall of 1895, the **Abram Smith** spent most of her life working more obscure ports in the lumber trade.

Courtesy of Milwaukee Public Library

Seen here during the 1905 Holland stranding, The Argo's people **are being rescued,** the **Argo** was later re-floated **and** ran for many more years under the name **Racine**, and on salt water as **Rene'**.
Courtesy of The Great Lakes Historical Society

Long after most of her wooden counter parts had outlived their usefulness, the **Miami** continued to earn her way along the Saginaw River. A local boat with a hometown crew.
Courtesy of Milwaukee Public Library

Ship and Boat Index

ACKNOWLEDGEMENTS

There are a number of persons without whose input this book would have been hollow at best and the following is a brief list and giving of permanent thanks.

Great thanks to my wife, Teresa, who tired of my hunt-and-peck method of typing and took that task to heart speeding the book's completion by tenfold. Gratitude to John Getsy whose computer skill was of great help. Also, to Dr. Roger Osterholm and Steve Glassman (of Embry-Riddle Aeronautical University's Humanities department) whose candid criticism and input aided in the author's style development. Thanks also to Ben Brennan who aided in computer magic.

Special thanks to Adeline Heilbronn whose careful keeping of her family history was of great help. To Chief Russell Pank whose grand tour of American Steamship Company's <u>Sam Laud</u> expanded my knowledge of the modern self-unloader. Gratitude also to Captain Don Ghiata for his below zero tour of the <u>S. T. Crapo</u> and summer tour of the <u>E. M. Ford</u>, and for just being an all around nice guy. Gratitude to Kathy McGraw of the Great Lakes Maritime Institute for photos and leads.

Then there are the people at the grassroots of this text's development, most prominently David M. "Bullet" Willett, whose passion for anything that floats and collection of information was of great help. Also, D. J. Story who is one of the Great Lakes' fastest rising young vessel photographers, a true artist who has yet to be discovered. Thanks to the librarians at the Bay City Branch Library, who put up with me as I ran their micro-film copy machines out of paper, developer and toner. And last, but not nearly least, my family: My brother Craig, an outstanding writer if I do say so, and my dad, mom and sister who put up with me on constant trips of great expense to the Soo. To all of these people and some I may have forgotten, thank you.

About the Author

W. Wes Oleszewski was born in Saginaw, Michigan in 1957. His fascination with the big lake boats grew up with him as they often crossed paths along the Saginaw River. In 1977, he began to study Great Lakes maritime history as a hobby; this included starting a resource library, developing a photo collection, and constructing a fleet of radio controlled lakers. He joined the Great Lakes Maritime Institute in 1982 and the Saginaw River Marine Historical Society in 1988.

A 1988 Graduate of Embry-Riddle Aeronautical University, Wes earned a Bachelor of Science Degree in Aeronautical Science. He holds a commercial pilot certificate and instrument rating for multi-engine aircraft as well as flight instructor ratings. He is currently engaged in a career as a professional pilot.

PLEASE RETURN TO:

Avery Color Studios
Star Route - Box 275
Au Train, Michigan 49806
Phone: (906) 892-8251
IN MICHIGAN
CALL TOLL FREE
1-800-722-9925

Your complete shipping address:

____

____

____

Fold, Staple, Affix Stamp and Mail ____________

____

____

____

______

Avery COLOR STUDIOS
Star Route - Box 275
AuTrain, Michigan 49806